THE CORPORATE PROFESSOR

DR. TUHIN S BANERJEE

"Dedicated to all my esteemed faculty, supportive colleagues, and eager students who have been my pillars of strength throughout this journey. A special acknowledgment to Prof. D Nagabrahmam, whose unwavering belief in my abilities has been a guiding light.

To my beloved daughters Priyanka and Priyasha, whose meticulous proofreading ensured the polish of every page. To my dear friend Vijay Pereira, whose insightful foreword adds depth to these pages.

To my loving wife Sumitra, whose unwavering support has been my rock. And to my mother, whose unwavering belief in me has been my driving force. Thank you all for being a part of this adventure."

Contents

Foreword

Tuhin (Dr Banerjee) is my classmate, and we have known each other for over 50 years now. Oops just let out that we are ancient. A few moons ago in Bangalore, I invited Tuhin to two of my book launches, and lo and behold, today, I pen a foreword for his book. Like him, I too made a transition into academia from the other side, so Deja vu!! What a fantastic story, though, that Tuhin has narrated; the context, the structure, and the content are just amazing and captivating.

Chapter one, what Tuhin calls a 'downshift' is really a great choice of transition for 'greater things in life' for him. I say this because Tuhin, has been a class topper all through school, and a house captain, a real all-rounder, and a role model to all of us! Corporate's loss was academia's gain, really. So, in reality and in all honesty, chapter two is losing the tie and doing justice to the chalk! An intelligent decision by an intellect!

'Baptism by fire' it was in chapters three (finding oneself in academia) and chapter four, where he learns from his family (daughters) on how to deal with the new generation of students. Welcome to academia, Tuhin; we learn every day! We are lifelong learners!

Chapter five to ten just portray the matrix structure that an academic has to manage and balance. Teaching is only part of one's academic career. Research, administrative work and constant innovation and creativity are required to not only be successful, but to even survive. Tuhin (Hemant) had identified the key skills needed for academics in today's world. How to navigate through terms, student engagement, exams, group work, case studies, grading et al. Bravo!

Chapters eleven and twelve sum up the 'calling' and 'legacy' of academics who really strive to make a difference in the future of our societies and communities, the students. Well done Tuhin aka Hemant!

The 12 chapters thus roll through with finesse and great imagination. Just surreal! And so simply and artfully narrated too. A must read I recommend.

And as Rani says at the end of the book "To new beginnings, unpredictable markets, and life's uncharted ventures!" To greater heights and experiences dear Tuhin.

Dr. Vijay Pereira

(Distinguished Professor of International and Strategic Human Capital Management at NEOMA Business School).

Preface

This novel is a work of fiction. Names, characters, businesses, places, events, and incidents are either the products of my imagination or used in a fictitious manner. Any resemblance to actual persons, living or dead, or actual events is purely coincidental.

In this story, we follow the journey of a finance professor transitioning from a successful corporate career to academia. While the narrative may draw inspiration from real-life experiences and industry practices, it is important to note that this novel is a work of fiction. The characters and events are crafted to create a compelling story and are not intended to depict any specific individual or situation.

As readers embark on this literary journey, it is my hope that they will immerse themselves in the world of the protagonist, appreciating the challenges and triumphs that come with such a significant career shift. Through this story, I aim to entertain, inspire, and provoke thought, but above all, to provide an engaging narrative that stands on its own as a work of fiction.

Dr. Tuhin S. Banerjee

Acknowledgements

"The Corporate Professor" is the culmination of my own experiences as a faculty member, and it would not have been possible without the support and inspiration from numerous individuals.

I am deeply grateful to my students, whose feedback and interactions have been invaluable. They allowed me to understand the viewpoints of students, and their insights greatly enriched the narrative of this novel.

The stories and experiences shared by my colleagues have added depth and interest to the novel, making it more relatable and engaging. Their camaraderie and shared experiences have been a cornerstone in shaping this book.

To my friends, who always believed in my teaching abilities and encouraged me to explore innovative methods, your unwavering faith has been a driving force behind this endeavor.

A special thanks to my daughters, Priyanka and Priyasha, who shared their student experiences with me daily. Their stories and insights helped me capture the nuances of student life authentically.

To my wife, who always gets excited about my new books but humorously refuses to read them, your enthusiasm and support mean the world to me.

And finally, to my mother, who dotes on me and takes immense pride in my achievements, your love and encouragement have been my constant source of strength.

Thank you all for being a part of this journey. Happy Reading!

Dr. Tuhin S Banerjee

CHAPTER ONE

BOARDROOMS TO CLASSROOMS: THE GREAT DOWNSHIFT

Once upon a modern time, in the high-rise jungle of corporate warfare, I, a knight in shining Park Avenue, was unceremoniously dethroned from my lofty boardroom seat. Oh, how the mighty spreadsheet warrior fell! One day, I was orchestrating mergers like a maestro; the next, I was as relevant as a floppy disk at an Apple convention.

But despair not, for my tale is not one of woe but of whimsy! As I sat in my executive chair (now a relic in my living room), an epiphany struck me with the subtlety of a pie to the face. Why not trade my pinstripes for tweed and venture into the hallowed halls of academia?

Five Anecdotes Made Me Leave My Couch for the Unknown:

Anecdote 1: The Talking Fridge Incident

I knew it was time to move when my fridge started giving me life advice. Every time I opened it, a little voice seemed to say, "Is this all there is?" I realized it was just the whir of the motor, but when your appliances start questioning your life choices, it's a sign.

Anecdote 2: The Great Sofa Summit

My sofa and I had become such good friends that I named it 'Yaar'. While nestled in Yaar's plush embrace one evening, I found an old fortune cookie under a cushion. It read, "Change is coming." I decided it was either move out or start paying rent for my furniture.

Anecdote 3: The Balcony Squirrel Debacle

I had a balcony standoff with a squirrel named 'Chota Bhim'. 'Chota Bhim' was bold, daring, and had an unhealthy obsession with my potted plants. Watching him conquer his tiny world inspired me. If Chota Bhim could brave the unknown for a few nuts, surely, I could for new experiences.

Anecdote 4: The Jogging Epiphany

I went jogging once – just once. As I wheezed and stumbled around the park, a kid zoomed past me on a scooter, yelling, "You can do it, slow-moving man!" That kid was my accidental guru. If I could survive public humiliation and sore calves, I could survive a move.

Anecdote 5: The Farewell Tour of Misery

My 'farewell tour' of the office neighborhood included a visit to a café where the barista always got my name wrong. I'd miss being called 'Hem' (my name is Hemant). These small, comically tragic moments made me realize the joy of starting anew.

These small, comically tragic moments made me realize the joy of change.

As I packed my life into boxes, I realized that my motivation to move wasn't just about seeking change but embracing the unknown with a sense of humor. Each comical misadventure in my old life wasn't a deterrent but a stepping stone, leading me to the next chapter. Plus, I was eager to meet new furniture and local wildlife. Who knows, maybe my next sofa will be named *'Dildaar'*.

I decided it was time to break the news to my family at dinner.

"Family," I began with a dramatic pause, fork mid-air, "I've decided to leave the corporate world and become an academic."

My wife, Rani, skilled in the art of eyebrow archery, raised one so high it nearly disappeared into her hairline. "Is this like the time you decided to become a vegan magician?" she asked, her voice laced with a memory of lentil parathas and unfortunate card tricks.

"No, no, this is different," I assured, while our daughters, Jui and Jia, exchanged glances that clearly said, 'Here we go again.'

Jia, ever the pragmatist, chimed in. "So, you'll exchange your business suits for elbow patches and tweed jackets?"

Jui, the dreamer, looked starry-eyed. "Does this mean you'll have summers off? Can we turn your office into a yoga studio?"

"I was thinking more about research, writing papers, inspiring young minds..." I trailed off, noticing Rani's expression hadn't changed. "And yes, there might be tweed involved."

Rani put down her fork. "Honey, do you even know what academicians do? Remember your 'Great Indian

Novel' phase?"

I cleared my throat, recalling the ten pages of a novel that were now serving as a makeshift coaster for my coffee mug.

"Okay, valid point. But I've given this a lot of thought. I could teach, publish articles, attend conferences in exotic locations..."

"You hate flying," Jia pointed out.

"And conferences," added Jui.

"True but think of the intellectual stimulation! The pursuit of knowledge!" I said, trying to rally their support with my enthusiasm.

Rani sighed, her eyebrow finally descending from orbit. "We'll support you, but no more vegan magic, okay?"

I grinned, relieved. "Deal. No more vegan magic."

As we resumed eating, I couldn't help but feel excited about tweed jackets and elbow patches. The path ahead might be unknown, but at least it wouldn't involve late-night conference calls.

And so, I embarked on my scholarly crusade. Imagine a former corporate titan attending Train The Trainer Programs, where the biggest merger was between my patience and endless introductions to educational jargon. I swapped board meetings for Role Plays Sessions, where "leveraging synergies" turned into deciphering texts that even Google seemed to scratch its head at.

I started taking Guest Lectures at a new private university. Training, I soon discovered, was like presenting to investors, but with a livelier audience (students occasionally woke up). My PowerPoint skills, once used to hypnotize stakeholders into submission, now sparked life into topics like "The Economic Impact of Algo Trading on Indian Companies" – a metaphor I found strangely fitting for some of my former board meetings.

My guest lectures at the University were an adventure in themselves. Students queued up with queries ranging from deeply philosophical to "Will this be on the test?". I traded my once-feared executive assistant for an overly enthusiastic teaching assistant who considered color-coded filing systems as the height of excitement.

But, lo and behold, academia had its perks. Where else could you spark young minds, engage in intellectual duels, and still have time for an unhurried cup of coffee? I reveled in the gasps as I shared war stories from the corporate frontlines, now serving as cautionary tales or, on good days, motivational anecdotes.

In the end, losing my board position was like accidentally deleting a tense email: initially horrifying but ultimately liberating. The hallowed halls of academia, with their blend of youthful energy and timeless wisdom, offered a new kingdom for me to explore – armed not with spreadsheets and stock options but with knowledge and a newfound appreciation for the simple joy of training.

After completion of one semester of teaching, I was invited by Dean Monjolika for a discussion. I have become the sought-after Corporate Trainer known for turning dull seminars into comedy shows. I felt a little nervous as I waited outside the Dean's Office.

I was aware that Dean Monjolika, a stoic figure in the academic world, hadn't always been confined to the ivy-covered walls of academia. Once a fiery entrepreneur, she had built and sold a successful startup before the age of

30. However, a personal crisis, a desire for stability, and her love for education had steered her towards academia. Yet, deep down, the embers of her adventurous spirit still smoldered. As I entered her office, adorned with diplomas and awards, it seemed too small for our two towering egos.

"Hemant, we've seen what you can do," Dean Monjolika began, steepling her fingers like a movie villain. "How about we make this relationship more... permanent?"

I leaned back, feigning surprise. "A tenure? Are you sure the school is ready for my brand of education? I mean, I teach with memes and YouTube videos."

Dean Monjolika chuckled. "I believe the students call it 'relatable content.' And we need a bit of that around here. Our Investment Management course currently has the excitement level of getting a root canal done."

"Investment Management", I mused. "Well, I suppose I could spice it up. We'll start with the investment dilemma of whether to have pineapple on paratha in the canteen".

The Dean laughed, her usual stoicism slipping. "You will be recommended for the interview process, but on one condition. No pineapple Parathas. It's the real investment dilemma of our times."

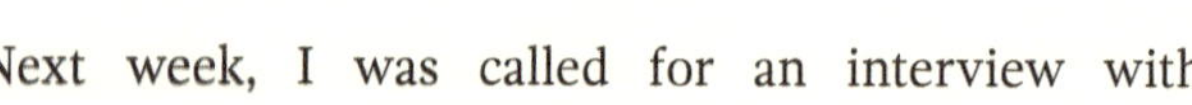

Next week, I was called for an interview with the University's Vice Chancellor.

I, Professor Hemant Banerjee, a titan in the corporate world, with more wrinkles than a well-traveled map and a wit sharper than a fencer's foil, found myself seated across from Vice Chancellor Iyer, a woman whose demeanor was as formidable as her academic credentials, which, rumor had it, were long enough to wallpaper the halls of the venerable institution she presided over.

"So, Professor Banerjee, after three decades of corporate crusades, what brings you to the tranquil – and considerably less lucrative – pastures of academia?" Iyer inquired, peering over her glasses with a mix of skepticism and curiosity.

I leaned back, a smile playing at the corners of my lips. "Well, Vice Chancellor, at my age, one starts to prefer the scent of old books over the smell of fresh investment reports. Besides, I've always fancied the idea of molding young minds, rather than just corporate strategies."

Iyer's eyebrow arched slightly, a silent, impressed acknowledgement. "I see. And how do you plan to engage these young minds? Our students are more tech-savvy than the IT Professionals in Naama Bengaluru"

"Ah," I chuckled, "I plan to teach them that not all wisdom can be Googled. "Some of it," I tapped my temple, "is right here, in the gray hardware."

The interview continued a delightful tango of wit and wisdom, leaving Iyer with a rare sense of anticipation. Perhaps this corporate mogul turned academic might just be a breath of fresh air needed to stir the hallowed halls of the university.

As I strolled out of the VC's office, my steps light with a sense of purpose renewed; I couldn't help but think, "From the boardroom to the blackboard – let the real education begin."

My next interview was scheduled soon. I, Professor Hemant Banerjee, PhD, esteemed in my own mind more than others, stood at the precipice of a career-defining moment - my interview with the University's Trust Member, Mr. Prakash Kamath. Mr. Kamath, known for his sharp wit and sharper spectacles, was the gatekeeper to the hallowed halls of academia.

As I entered the room, I was immediately struck by the imposing library surrounding them, books leaping from the shelves as if eager to join in the conversation. Mr. Kamath sat behind a desk that could easily double as a Viking longship, peering at me over his half-moon glasses with a gaze that suggested he had dissected more egos than he had dissertations.

"Professor Banerjee, so glad you could join us," he began, his voice as smooth as the polished oak of his desk. "I trust you found the labyrinth we call a campus without much trouble?"

"Indeed, Mr. Kamath," I replied, trying to match his tone. "I consider navigating academic complexities one of my specialties, both metaphorically and, as of today, literally."

A ghost of a smile touched his lips, as fleeting as a professor's promise of a 'light' reading assignment.

"So, tell me, Professor, about your research. I understand it involves the intricate investment rituals of the Lesser Spotted Venture Capitalist?" His tone was innocent, but his eyes sparkled with mischief.

I, warming to the challenge, launched into an enthusiastic explanation filled with vivid descriptions and the occasional overly dramatic hand gesture. "The Investment of the Venture Capitalist, Mr. Kamath, is a marvel of nature. The Entrepreneur struts and preens, puffing out his feathers like a young lecturer trying to impress. The Venture Capitalist, discerning and aloof, watches with a critical eye, deciding if his display is worthy of her seed capital."

"Ah, so rather similar to our academic selection process, then?" he quipped, his smirk threatening to become a full-fledged grin.

"Quite so," I chuckled. "Although, I must say, the VCs generally don't require a curriculum vitae."

Our conversation continued, weaving through the realms of academia with the grace of a well-rehearsed waltz. I found myself admiring Mr. Kamath's intellect and his ability to dart from subject to subject with the agility of a well-read hummingbird.

As the interview drew to a close, I realized I had not just survived the encounter but had thoroughly enjoyed it. Mr. Kamath extended his hand, his eyes twinkling with unspoken approval. "Professor Banerjee, it's been a delight. We shall be in touch, and HR will mail you the offer. And do watch out for the minotaur on your way out – the labyrinth can be quite unforgiving."

As I stepped out of the room, I couldn't help but feel like I had just participated in a pitch as intricate and fascinating as those of my beloved Venture Capitalists.

In my family's cozy, book-lined dining room, I was preparing for a critical presentation with my tweed jacket and the kind of bespectacled gaze that seemed to calculate your net worth at a glance. It wasn't for my seasoned corporate participants or a hall of eager students but for my most discerning audience yet: my family.

My wife Rani, whose art studio was a kaleidoscope of colors and canvases, watched me with an artist's critical eye. Our daughters, Jui, with her wildflower hair and passion for environmental causes, and Jia, whose fingers danced over her tablet like a pianist, were already formulating their positions.

As the aroma of butter chicken wafted from the oven, I unveiled my meticulously prepared charts. "Pathsala University isn't just a job opportunity; it's the Dalal Street of academia!"

Rani, sipping her green tea, remarked wryly, "Does this Pathsala have a gallery, or are its aesthetics limited to pie charts?"

Jui, her fork playing with her food, interjected, "What about the environmental impact, Dad? Your new commute equals more carbon emissions."

Jia, barely looking up, added, "And I checked their BBA program. It's still teaching License Raj in the AI Age."

Their comments hit me like unexpected market fluctuations. I hadn't anticipated such resistance. My mind raced back to my own university days, a scholarship student in a sea of affluence, determined to make my mark. Pathsala was my dream, a pinnacle I never thought attainable.

Seeing my hesitation, Rani's expression softened. "Hemant, we just want to ensure this move aligns with your dreams and ours too."

The room was steeped in a moment of reflection. My gaze settled on my family, my most valuable investment. "What if we all visit Pathsala? Meet the people and see the campus. If it doesn't feel right for any of us, I won't take the position."

A new dialogue began, including possibilities, compromises, dreams, and realities. It was more intricate and beautiful than any financial model I had ever created. In the laughter and chatter that followed, I found my heart swelling with a richness that no salary could match. I realized that in the grand ledger of life, these moments truly balanced the books.

I remember the day quite distinctly. I received the offer to join the faculty of Pathsala University. The offer, penned in the most elegant script, lay on my mahogany desk, flanked by stacks of financial journals and a calculator that had seen better days.

Now, the decision to transition wasn't purely a matter of economics. As they say in finance, 'non-monetary factors' were at play. My family had reservations, and I had doubts like a cautious investor eyeing a startup. It wasn't the salary; no, our concerns were more... shall we say, environmental?

Thus, our family visited the University after gaining an appointment with the HR head of the University. We were welcomed by Mr. Prem Chopra, the HR head of the University, a man whose efficiency could put the Swiss railways to shame. In our meeting, I posed the questions that nagged at our family like unpaid dividends.

"Mr. Prem, what of the office space? In my current position, I've grown accustomed to a certain... cubic footage."

He smiled, the kind of smile that could disarm a corporate raider. "Dr. Banerjee, rest assured, your office will not only be spacious but also offer a splendid view of our historic campus. Think of it as a corner office on Dalal Street, minus the traffic noise."

"And the students?" I inquired. "I've heard tales of their... modern attitudes."

"Think of it as diversifying your portfolio," he quipped. "A range of perspectives that will only enrich your academic experience. Plus, I've seen your lecture ratings; you're practically a blue-chip stock in the academic world."

I must admit, his words had a comforting effect, like a well-diversified portfolio. Mr. Chopra seemed to anticipate my concerns with the precision of a well-calculated forecast.

"And research opportunities?" I added, trying to sound nonchalant.

"Our university offers unparalleled support for research," he said confidently. "We're like venture capitalists for academic pursuits. You bring the ideas; we provide the resources. I shall email you all the details"

By the end of our meeting, our doubts had evaporated like market fears after a reassuring RBI announcement. The decision was clear. I would accept the offer, diversify my academic holdings, and embark on this new venture with the enthusiasm of a bullish market.

Pathsala University, a prestigious university renowned for its ivy-covered walls and coffee-stained financial journals, had extended me an offer to join their ranks. The offer, elegant in its wording, was akin to a siren song for me, promising a world where numbers danced, and stocks serenaded.

As I pondered this proposal, an email from the university's HR department buzzed into my inbox, marked urgent and important. Intrigued, I opened it, only to find a list of additional clarifications that seemed to be more befuddling than the most complex financial derivatives.

First, they clarified that my office would be "cozy." An aficionado of euphemisms, I interpreted this as "You'll be lucky to swing a cat." I pictured a broom closet armed with an ancient computer and a chair that squeaked in protest at every budget forecast.

Second, the email mentioned a "dynamic parking situation." I chuckled, envisaging a daily treasure hunt for a parking spot, likely culminating in a brisk walk from the next suburb.

The third point elucidated the "collaborative teaching approach" of the university. With a twinkle in my eye, I imagined tag-teaming with the janitorial staff to explain the intricacies of fiscal policy.

Lastly, the email highlighted the "vibrant student engagement" I could expect. Translated from HR speak, I foresaw a future of spirited debates, where every lecture might end with "But in the real world, Professor..."

Despite these clarifications, or perhaps because of them, I felt a surge of excitement. I envisaged myself not just as a purveyor of financial wisdom but as a navigator in the choppy waters of academic quirks. The challenges presented were not deterrents but rather spices that would flavor my daily routine.

With a smile, I drafted my acceptance. I looked forward to my cozy office, dynamic parking adventures, collaborative teaching escapades, and vibrant student interactions. For me, this was more than a job offer; it was an invitation to a grand adventure in the world of academia, where the balance sheets were as unpredictable as the students I would teach.

And so, with a witty quip at the ready and a ledger under my arm, I set forth into my new chapter, ready to account for every unexpected joy and peculiar predicament that academia had to offer.

I wrote back "I accept the offer and I will join from the 1st of next month".

CHAPTER TWO

The Art of Losing the Tie (and Finding the Chalk)

As I stepped into the hallowed halls of the esteemed Pathsala University on the day of joining, my heart pounded with a rhythm that could rival the stock market's most erratic day. There I was, a professor of finance, my brain teeming with formulas and theories, ready to enlighten young minds about the enthralling world of assets and liabilities.

The HR department, a realm where smiles were as scarce as a bad investment in my portfolio, was my first checkpoint. The HR head, Mr. Prem Chopra, greeted me with a handshake that felt like a merger agreement. He handed me a mountain of forms to fill out; each page dripped with bureaucratic enthusiasm.

"Please fill these out. And don't forget to calculate your personal tax liabilities correctly. We expect our finance faculty to lead by example!" Mr. Chopra said with a smirk that hinted he enjoyed this little irony more than he should.

As I scribbled my way through the paperwork, I couldn't help but ponder the irony. Here I was, about to teach the nuances of financial complexities, yet struggling to decode the hieroglyphics of HR forms. Mr. Chopra watched me like a hawk overseeing its investment portfolio, ensuring I didn't miss a single line.

Finally, after what felt like an audit session, I was declared financially fit to teach. Mr. Chopra shook my hand again, "Welcome to Pathsala University. My assistant Mrs. Roopa will show you around. Remember, no insider trading of exam papers!"

As I exited the room, his laughter echoing down the hallway, I couldn't help but smile. My journey in the world of academia had begun not with a lecture but with a real-life lesson in finance – navigating the bureaucratic balance sheets of the HR department.

As a newly joined Finance Professor, my first day at the university was less of a gentle introduction and more of a whirlwind tour in the company of Mrs. Roopa, our unflappably enthusiastic HR guide. Mrs. Roopa, armed with a clipboard that I suspect was bolted to her hand at birth, whisked me through corridors with the efficiency of a Dalal Street trader closing deals.

Our first stop was the Economics Department, a realm where supply and demand were not just concepts but a way of life. This place I hoped, was going to write my favorable destiny. The corridor was lined with portraits of eminent economists, each looking more serious than the last. I imagined my portrait joining them one day, perhaps with a slightly more approachable expression. I was introduced to Professor Adam, whose handshake was as firm as his reputation for making students cry during finals. "Welcome to the jungle," he said with a grin that suggested he enjoyed the metaphor a little too much.

Roopa's commentary was a mix of useful information and university lore as we walked. "And this," she said, pointing to a seemingly unremarkable door, "is the infamous 'Supply Closet'. Legend has it that an econ professor once walked in and re-emerged a year later with a groundbreaking paper on resource allocation."

I chuckled. "Was the paper titled 'The Optimal Use of Space and Time'?"

Roopa laughed. "You'll fit right in here; let's show your department!"

Our next stop was the Finance Department. As I admired the Bloomberg Terminals, I noted the air of seriousness that hung over the room like a heavy balance sheet. Students were engrossed in their data analysis, their expressions fluctuating with the stock market trends they were probably tracking.

"Here, emotions are bearish, and bull markets reign supreme," I quipped.

Roopa nodded sagely. "Just don't mention cryptocurrency volatility around here; it's a sensitive topic."

Next, we ventured into the Marketing Department, where the scent of freshly printed case studies hung in the air like a new product's perfume. Here, I met Professor Nirma, who regarded me over the rim of her glasses with a look that seemed to calculate my net worth. "I hope you're good with numbers," she quipped, "because even the coffee machine requires a cost-benefit analysis around here."

As we continued our odyssey, Mrs. Roopa provided a running commentary punctuated with what I assumed was supposed to be humorous asides about the various administrative quirks of the university. For instance, I learned that the third floor copier was named 'Hema Malini' and was prone to jamming if not sweet-talked properly.

As I continued exploring the manicured lawns of the university, my mind was a ledger of expectations and anxieties, neatly balanced. The university, renowned for its illustrious finance program and notorious for its labyrinthine corridors, awaited me.

Finally, we arrived at the office of my new boss, the Dean of the Business School. Her office was a shrine to the free market, complete with a miniature bird on her desk. The Dean, a woman whose smile was as tight as her budget, greeted me with a nod that seemed to appraise my academic credentials and market value again simultaneously.

"So, you have been brave to join our ranks," she began, her voice as smooth as a stock ticker. "I hope you're ready to invest your talents here. Just remember, in this market, we expect a high return on investment."

As I left her office, feeling a little like a stock that had just been publicly traded, I realized that my journey in the world of academia would be as unpredictable as the stock market. But, like any good investor, I was ready for the challenge, armed with knowledge, wit, and a newfound appreciation for university-level bureaucracy.

"Let's get you acquainted with the remaining of our little kingdom!" said Mrs. Roopa

Finally, we arrived at the crown jewel of any academic institution – the canteen. The aroma of coffee was stronger than any market force I'd encountered. Students and faculty were engaged in heated debates, likely over

Keynesian economics versus Classical theories or perhaps just over the last slice of pepperoni pizza.

"This," Mrs. Roopa declared, "is where real policies are debated, Professor. Also, they make a mean paneer sandwich."

As our tour concluded, we proceeded to my office. I felt a curious blend of inspiration and hunger – for knowledge and possibly for one of those paneer sandwiches. My first day at university was less about finance and more about finding my place in this delightful tapestry of academia.

We arrived at what was to be my sanctuary of spreadsheets, my haven of hedge funds – my office. The room was an eclectic mix of academic austerity and unintentional comedy. The desk stood proudly in the center, a robust relic from the era when ledger books weighed more than the accountants lifting them. A computer, no doubt chosen for its ability to crunch numbers rather than its speed, sat atop it, winking its single blinking light as if in anticipation of fiscal forecasts.

"The last professor," Mrs. Roopa explained with a mischievous grin, "left in a hurry. Something about the stock market and a bad sandwich at lunch. Never quite got the full story."

The bookshelf was a testament to financial theories of yore, with titles like 'The Art of Amortization' and 'Fiscal Fantasies: A Love Story.' I half expected to find a hidden tome titled 'Where to Hide Your Money When Auditors Come Knocking.'

As I settled into my new academic abode, I couldn't help but feel a sense of excitement. In this room, I would unravel the mysteries of money, decode the enigmas of economics, and perhaps find the perfect formula for my coffee to prevent the budget meeting snooze-fests.

The day continued with introductions to colleagues, a tour of the mini cafeteria (Mrs. Roopa insisting that the Mini Samosas was a 'calculated risk'), and a brief meeting with the Vice Chancellor, a woman whose handshake was as firm as her leave policies.

As the day drew to a close, I reflected on the journey ahead. The world of finance was ever-changing, but I was ready to chart its course, armed with ledgers, laughter, and a little bit of economic magic.

And to think, this was just the orientation. I couldn't wait for the semester to begin, where balance sheets and budget reports would be my tools and shaping bright financial minds would be my trade. With some luck, I might even find that mythical 'Supply Closet' and emerge with a groundbreaking theory of my own – preferably before lunchtime.

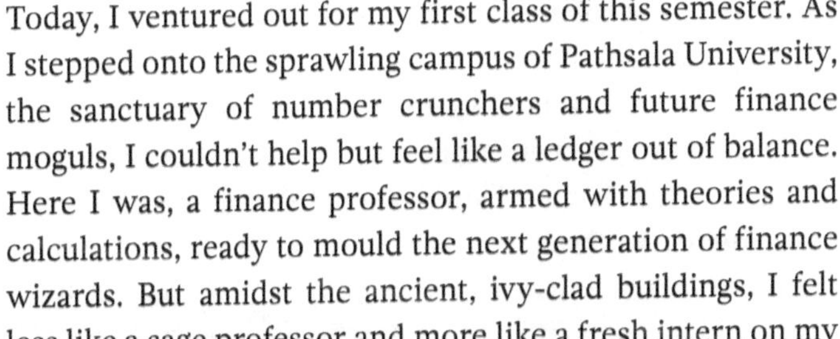

Today, I ventured out for my first class of this semester. As I stepped onto the sprawling campus of Pathsala University, the sanctuary of number crunchers and future finance moguls, I couldn't help but feel like a ledger out of balance. Here I was, a finance professor, armed with theories and calculations, ready to mould the next generation of finance wizards. But amidst the ancient, ivy-clad buildings, I felt less like a sage professor and more like a fresh intern on my first day on Dalal Street.

My first encounter was with the campus map – a cryptic document requiring more analytical skills than a complex financial report. I meandered through the maze of buildings, passing by students who were engrossed in conversations that ranged from the latest AI buzz to the eternal question of where to find the best coffee on campus. Finally, after a journey that felt like a rite of passage, I located the Finance Building, a stately structure that looked as if it was designed by Sharpe himself.

I, Dr Hemant Banerjee, whose name once echoed through the marble halls of the top Investment Company in India, was on the threshold of an entirely different world. Room 203 of the Pathsala School of Business looked nothing like the boardrooms I was accustomed to, filled instead with the vibrant chatter of BBA students, who viewed neckties as ancient relics and 'profit margins' as good names for rock bands. As I stepped in, I felt the weight of my glossy, leather briefcase – a stark contrast to the canvas backpacks slung over the shoulders of my youthful audience.

Unlike the muted tones and imposing oak tables of the boardrooms I was used to, this classroom buzzed with the energy of youth. Sunlight spilled through large windows, casting a warm glow on rows of utilitarian desks, each adorned with a colorful array of stickers, water bottles, and digital paraphernalia.

The students, a medley of disheveled hair and casual attire, lounged in their seats with the easy confidence of digital natives. Some chatted animatedly about the latest viral meme, while others were lost in the glow of their laptop screens, only occasionally glancing up as if to confirm they were still, in fact, in a classroom. One student, wearing a t-shirt that boldly proclaimed, 'Finance is my love language,' chewed on a pencil while scrolling through what looked suspiciously like a dating app.

"Good morning," I said, voice imbued with a corporate gravitas that seemed to bounce off the walls and land nowhere in particular. The response was a mosaic of half-hearted murmurs and the continued tapping of smartphone keyboards.

I cleared my throat, glancing down at my meticulously prepared notes. They suddenly seemed like transcripts from another era. I looked up, meeting the student's gaze in the front row, whose expression hovered between amusement and curiosity. My tie, a meticulously chosen silver-grey piece, felt like a noose rather than a symbol of authority.

At that moment, I realized that the lessons I planned to teach about finance management were perhaps not the only lessons I might learn in return. I took a deep breath and attempted my first connection with this new audience. "When I started in the business world," I began my voice a relic of boardroom battles past. The response was a mixture of polite smiles and curious glances. One student in the back, his hair a rebellious shade of blue, raised an eyebrow in a silent challenge.

My fingers fumbled as I reached for the chalk, unaccustomed to such archaic instruction tools. The chalk snapped in two, causing a soft chuckle to ripple through the class. My face flushed, but as I looked up, I was met not with scorn but a gentle, albeit amused, empathy. It was then I realized that my journey at Pathsala wasn't just about teaching profit margins and market strategies but also about embracing a world far removed from the one I knew. With a half-smile, I began loosening my tie, letting it hang loosely as I picked up another piece of chalk. As I introduced myself, I accidentally switched on the wrong presentation, filling the screen with pictures from my recent Thailand trip.

A student shouted from the back, "Guess finance really is about the 'net' gains, huh?" causing an eruption of laughter.

Trying to recover, I dive into my lecture. I start discussing the difference between fixed and current assets. While illustrating my point, I accidentally knock over my water, spilling it over my notes.

While I scramble to save the papers, a girl quips, "Looks like your assets are pretty liquid today, Professor." Another student, seizing the opportunity, broadcasts a quick meme he created onto the screen, showing me Scuba Diving with the caption, "Liquidating the assets."

The class bursts into laughter again, including the Class Representative, who then helps me organize my wet papers. The front-bencher, eager to redirect the focus, raises a hand and asks an advanced question about Asset Reconstruction funds. I, grateful for the change in topic, delved into a detailed explanation, which goes over most students' heads, but another student offers a simple analogy, making it easier for the class to understand.

As the class ends, I was a bit embarrassed but amused. "Let's take the attendance."' I said.

The true adventure began with a seemingly mundane task – taking attendance. Ah, attendance, that rudimentary roll call which, in the hands of a room full of Bengaluru's best and brightest, transformed into a scene straight out of a Rohit Shetty's film.

Armed with a list of names and a determination to pronounce each correctly, I commenced the roll call. "Pari," I began, to which a voice from the back responded, "Present, but perpetually absent in spirit, Professor." The class erupted in laughter. I chuckled along, appreciating the candor.

"Bhanu Anna?" I continued. "Here, but I'm just Bhanu today, Professor. Anna's my alter ego on weekends." More chuckles. The atmosphere was undeniably infectious.

"Leena?" A hand shot up, followed by a solemn declaration, "Present, but currently questioning the existential purpose of derivative markets." The class was now in stitches, and despite my best efforts to maintain a professorial demeanor, I was thoroughly enjoying this unexpected comedy hour.

With each name, the responses grew more inventive. "Rohit Sharma?" prompted a chorus of "He is captaining the Indian cricket team!" A Cricket reference – these students were as sports savvy as they were financially astute.

The pièce de résistance arrived with the call of "Manmohan Singh." A pause ensued, filled by a distant voice, "Present, and also the 13th Prime Minister of India in my spare time." The room burst into an uproar of laughter, and I couldn't help but join in.

I thanked the students for an 'eventful' first class. I remarked, "Well, this was an interesting start. Looking forward to more 'financial adventures' with you all.

The students left, chatting and laughing, with one student joking, "Can't wait for our next Diving Expedition in finance!"

In this session, I learned the names and faces of a few of my new students and the importance of humor and patience in teaching. Initially just a mandatory course for many, the class began to feel more like a community, eager to see what the next class held.

I, hoping to create a more relaxed and engaging atmosphere after my eventful first class, decided to start the next session with student introductions. I thought it was a great way to break the ice and get to know my students better.

A few Introductions stood out for me:

Arjun: "Hi, I'm Arjun. I'm majoring in finance and have read all your published papers, Professor. I especially enjoyed your article on..." Arjun continues to list my achievements until I gently cut in, joking, "Thank you, Arjun. I'm glad at least someone's reading them!"

Pari: "Pari here. I'm only in this class because it's mandatory. I don't have much interest in finance - unless it's about financing my Maggie addiction." I laughed and replied, "Well, Pari, let's see if we can make finance as exciting as a Maggie rush!"

Bhanu: "Hey, I'm Bhanu. Honestly, I'm more into tech and coding, but I'm here to learn how finance can be revolutionized with technology." I intrigued said, "That's a valuable perspective, Bhanu. Maybe you can help digitize my old-school notes!"

Leena: "I'm Leena. I took a break from my career to come back to school. I might ask a lot of questions, so bear with me!" I warmly responded, "Asking questions is how we learn, Leena. I'm sure your insights will benefit us all!"

Sagar: "Sagar's the name, and I'm probably the least financially knowledgeable person here. But hey, I can bring some laughs!" I smiled and said, "Every class needs some humor, Sagar. Just, maybe, save the best jokes for after class!"

I also noted the uniqueness of each of my students:

Arjun - The Overachiever: Arjun sat in the front row, always ready with a notebook. Eager to impress, Arjun often interrupts with complicated questions, sometimes derailing my lecture.

Pari - The Reluctant Student: Pari is in this class only because it's a requirement. She's often seen doodling in her notebook, paying minimal attention, and occasionally offering a sarcastic comment under her breath.

Bhanu - The Tech-Savvy Whiz: Always on his laptop, Bhanu seems more interested in coding or designing on his screen than in financial management. However, he has a knack for linking financial concepts to tech trends.

Leena - The Group Mom: Leena is a mature student returning to education. She's organized and caring, and I often saw her helping others with notes or explaining concepts in a simpler way.

Sagar - The Clown: Sagar sat at the back, always ready with a joke. He's popular among his peers for his light-hearted approach and never misses a chance to crack a joke, often at the most inopportune moments.

This was the heterogeneous group that attended my class and sometimes bunked my classes.

With the introductions done, I dove into the intricacies of financial principles. I noticed a student in the back row, fervently typing away on his laptop. Assuming he was taking diligent notes, I felt a surge of professorial pride, only to discover later that he was actually trading stocks during my lecture. Talk about real-time application of classroom knowledge!

I began with what I thought was a rousing speech about the beauty of finance, only to be interrupted by a student in the front row who earnestly asked, "Is this going to be on the exam?" Ah, the eternal question that transcends all academic disciplines!

The highlight of my day came when discussing the concept of risk and return. To illustrate, I shared a personal story of my riskiest investment – betting on Royal Challengers Bangalore to win IPL23. The class erupted in laughter, and the gap between professor and student seemed to bridge just a bit at that moment.

My first week at Pathsala University was a blend of humor, humility, and learning curves steeper than a bullish stock chart. As I walked back through the campus, no longer a lost soul but a slightly more seasoned academic, I realized that while I may be there to teach finance, my students would teach me just as much about humor, adaptability, and the unexpected adventures of university life.

The next adventure was dealing with University Administration. As I strode confidently into the complex corridors of University's Business School, my aura exuded the gravitas of a seasoned financier, albeit one embarking on my first foray into the academic jungle. Armed with an arsenal of spreadsheets and compounded interest formulas, I was unprepared for the day's forthcoming comedic escapades.

On reaching the administration office, I was greeted by Ms. Helen, the school's administrative assistant, whose smile was as fixed and unwavering as the ancient typewriter she fiercely guarded. In a voice reminiscent of chalk scraping a blackboard, she informed me that the teaching aids I'd requested were akin to mythical creatures in the realm of the university's budget.

Undeterred, I produced a meticulously crafted PowerPoint presentation in the next class, my secret weapon to dazzle the freshmen with financial wizardry. Yet, in a plot twist worthy of a Greek tragedy, I discovered that the new classroom was only equipped with a chalkboard. My dreams of digital dazzle fizzled faster than a poorly leveraged hedge fund.

In an act of desperation, I scoured the campus for a projector, only to find myself entangled in a bureaucratic odyssey that made Ulysses' journey seem like a weekend getaway. From one department to another, I was passed around like a hot potato in a game played by Big Boss.

Just as I was about to admit defeat, I stumbled upon a dusty, antiquated projector in a forgotten storage closet. Triumphantly, I wheeled my newfound treasure to the classroom, only to realize I had no idea how to operate this relic from a bygone era.

As I grappled with the ancient projector, a small group of intrigued students gathered around. They watched as I fumbled, my usually confident demeanor dissolving into a mix of frustration and bemusement. It was then that a quiet student from the back, Emma, a tech-savvy finance major with a knack for old electronics, stepped forward.

"Professor, may I?" she asked, her voice a mixture of curiosity and confidence. With a nod from me, Emma began to tinker with the projector. Sensing an unusual learning opportunity, the other students gathered around, offering suggestions and searching for manuals online on their smartphones.

This unexpected teamwork turned the tide. The projector sputtered to life, casting a dim but triumphant light onto the chalkboard. Now humbly sharing the stage with Emma, I adapted my lecture on the fly. I intertwined the basics of finance with lessons on the value of resourcefulness and collaboration.

In the end, my lecture was a symphony of improvisation. I juggled chalk, anecdotes, and the few slides I managed to project upside down. The students, initially bewildered, were soon charmed by my unorthodox methods and palpable passion for finance.

As the class ended, the students applauded, not just for the knowledge gained but for the experience of turning a challenge into a collaborative success. I thanked Emma and the class, realizing that this day had taught me as much as I had taught my students.

As the day drew to a close, I reflected on my adventures. I realized that the most valuable lesson I taught that day was not found in any textbook: the art of adaptability in the face of chaos. And with that epiphany, I chuckled to myself, already plotting the next day's curriculum with a mischievous twinkle in my eye.

Once on a sunny afternoon, I faced an unexpected conundrum. Mid-lecture, like a candle snuffed out by a mischievous breeze, my voice vanished. The amphitheater, usually echoing with my passionate orations, fell into a silence so profound that one could hear a pen drop - and indeed, several did in astonishment.

What transpired next was a series of comical attempts to regain my voice, each more ludicrous than the last, as suggested by my loving yet decidedly eccentric family.

My wife, Rani, a believer in the mystical, suggested a concoction so bizarre it could have been a potion brewed in the depths of a fairy tale forest. It included, among other things, honey from bees who had only pollinated bluebells and the whispers of a willow tree. I, ever the dutiful husband, tried it, only to end up with a sticky beard and an even stickier situation.

My eldest daughter, Jui, recommended projecting my voice through the art of mime. Imagine, if you will, a distinguished professor gesticulating wildly, enacting the process of Investing without uttering a single word. My students were torn between bafflement and uncontrollable giggles. It was educational, yet it looked like a silent film about a confused investor.

My younger daughter, Jia, handed me a text-to-speech app. I, not the most adept with technology, made the app recite my lecture in a monotone robotic voice that somehow took on a life of its own, digressing into economic forecasts and random facts about investing.

In the end, my voice did return, not with a bang but with a whisper, just in time for me to conclude my lectures with a newfound appreciation for the spoken word. My students, meanwhile, had learned an unexpected lesson: there's more than one way to communicate, and sometimes, the most memorable lessons come from the most unexpected teachers.

After the mute classes, I retreated to the faculty lounge, seeking solace and maybe a remedy. My colleagues from various departments, always eager to lend their 'expert' advice, gathered around.

The Marketing Professor, Nirma, with a flashy grin, was the first to chime in. "Prof Banerjee, my friend, this is a golden opportunity! Imagine the buzz you'll create. We'll start a whisper campaign: 'The Silent Professor.' Students will flock to your lectures just for the novelty!"

I raised an eyebrow, unimpressed.

Next, the Economics Professor Adam leaned in, adjusting his glasses. "Consider this from a supply and demand perspective. Your silence has just made your words more valuable. Start a bidding war for written lectures. Finance 101!"

A soft groan escaped my lips.

Finally, the Psychology Professor Mamta, with a thoughtful nod, offered her view. "It's clear you're experiencing a psychosomatic response to stress. You need to visualize your voice as a free-flowing river. Embrace the silence, find your inner voice, and it will return."

I, now more confused than ever, sipped my coffee quietly, wondering if mime school was a viable career change. Why don't they provide microphones in the classrooms, I wondered!!!

Next day, armed with a blend of naiveté and determination, I approached the administration office. The room was a labyrinth of paperwork and unenthusiastic faces, seemingly unfazed by my urgent request.

"Excuse me, I need a microphone for my lecture this afternoon," I said, my voice barely rising above the air conditioner's hum.

Ms. Helen, a lady with glasses perched precariously at the tip of her nose, peered at me over the rim. "A microphone? Did you fill out form 27B/6?"

"Form 27B/6?" I echoed, my heart sinking.

"Yes, and it needs to be signed by the Dean," she said, returning to her typing.

The Dean, however, was a mythical creature, rarely seen and even more rarely approachable. After several hours of a wild goose chase, I finally cornered the elusive Dean in the cafeteria, Masala Dosa in hand.

"Ah, Professor Banerjee, the new finance wizard!" the Dean exclaimed, crumbs flying. "What can I do for you?"

I explained my predicament. After a hearty laugh, the Dean scribbled her signature on the form. Triumphantly, I returned to the administration office, only to be told, "The person in charge of the microphones is on lunch break. Come back in an hour."

As the clock ticked closer to my lecture, I again realized I had to improvise. Channeling the spirit of a stage actor, I projected my voice, articulating the wonders of financial theories without any technological aid. Surprisingly, my passion and the clarity of my voice reached even the students in the back row.

After the lecture, Leena approached me. "Sir, that was amazing! You made finance sound like an adventure!"

I smiled, realizing that sometimes, the best lessons are those taught without a script... or a microphone.

CHAPTER THREE

SURVIVING THE FIRST SEMESTER: THE CORPORATE PROFESSOR'S GUIDE TO 'COOL' SLANG

As I stood amidst the desolate aisles, a flashback whisked me away to just a month ago. I had been in my old study room at home, surrounded by stacks of well-thumbed books, telling my wife, Rani, about my new adventure. "Rani, I can't wait to dive into the depths of a grand university library. Imagine the first editions, the handwritten notes in the margins, the scent of wisdom in the air!"

Rani chuckled, "Just don't get lost in there, old man."

Now, the contrast couldn't be starker. Where I expected a sea of books, I found a desert. And in this desert, that lone computer stood like an oasis. Hesitantly, I approached, the click-clack of the keyboard replacing the familiar rustling of pages.

As I navigated through the digital archives, I marveled at the sheer volume of information at my fingertips. "Well, this is convenient," I mumbled to myself, a chuckle escaping my lips. "Rani would have a field day with this."

Clicking through articles, eBooks, and virtual seminars, I realized the essence of modern finance and academia. Here was a world where information was not bound by physical limitations, where the exchange of ideas was as rapid as the stock market's fluctuations.

In a way, this empty library and its single digital portal symbolized the evolution of my field. Finance was no longer just about ledgers and ticker tape; it had embraced the digital age with gusto. The irony was clear - as a finance professor, I needed to appreciate not just the value of assets but also the value of change and adaptation.

However, as fate would have it, my challenge continued in the maze of knowledge known as the university library.

I approached the librarian, Ms. Sarawati, a woman whose demeanor was as stern as her bun was tight. "Good morning," I stammered, "I'm Professor Banerjee. I need to order textbooks for my finance course... something that explains complex financial theories but doesn't cost as much as a minor hedge fund."

Ms. Sarawati peered at me over her glasses, a look that made me feel like a misplaced comma in an otherwise perfect sentence. "You're the new finance professor, then? We were expecting someone... taller."

Taken aback, I adjusted my tie, a futile effort to compensate for my height. "Well, I assure you, my knowledge of finance is quite... tall."

Ms. Sarawati cracked a smile, the first sign of warmth, like a reluctant sunrise. "Let's see what we have," she said, leading me through aisles that I was convinced were rearranging themselves just to confuse me.

As they walked, Ms. Sarawati quizzed him. "What's your take on the pricing of these new-age IPOs?"

Feeling more at ease, I launched into an explanation using metaphors involving books and bookshelves. When we reached the finance section, Ms. Sarawati looked thoroughly amused. "Well, Professor Banerjee, you do have a way with words. Not what I expected from someone who deals with numbers all day."

We selected the textbooks; I am grateful for the unexpected camaraderie. As I left, Ms. Sarawati called out, "Don't forget, Professor, in this library, every number has its story!"

I stepped out, textbooks in hand, feeling surprisingly at home. My story at the University appeared to be more interesting than any number could quantify.

In the grand annals of my academic career in the first semester, none would rival the infamous day when my expertise in finance met an audience as substantial as the sound of crickets on a moonlit night. I stood in the echoic chamber of Lecture Hall B-12, awaiting the eager minds of my Finance 101 class. The clock ticked, mirroring the rhythm of my expectant tapping foot.

By minute five, my anticipation had transformed into a spectacle of bewilderment. I peered over my half-moon glasses, surveying the empty rows. "An enthusiastic bunch," I mused, my voice bouncing off the walls, keeping company with my solitude. I imagined the students plotting this grand escapade, perhaps in the dimly lit corners of the university café, muffling their conspiratorial giggles with sips of overpriced coffee.

At minute ten, I considered the possibility of a natural disaster I hadn't heard of. Had there been an alien invasion? Surely, that would have made the morning news between the stock market updates and the weather forecast.

By the fifteenth minute, I started my lecture, addressing the void with the same fervor I would a packed hall. I expounded on the intricacies of corporate finance, pausing occasionally for effect or to field questions from the invisible attendees. My chalk danced across the blackboard, crafting elaborate graphs and formulas, a performance for an audience of none.

As I delved into the nuances of market fluctuations, I couldn't help but let my mind wander. I envisioned my students, now gallivanting across the campus, liberated from the shackles of compound interest and fiscal policy. "Ah, to be young and carefree," I sighed, my words a lone ship sailing across the sea of empty chairs.

The clock struck the hour, and I concluded my lecture with a customary, "Any questions?" The silence that followed was both an answer and a poignant reminder of my solitary vigil. I gathered my notes, my steps echoing in the deserted hall, a symphony of one. I noticed Sagar and Pari lurking in the corner; I chose to ignore them.

In the days that followed, the story of my solo lecture became the stuff of legend. Students whispered about the professor who taught a class to no one, a tale tinged with both admiration and mischief. For me, it was a moment of profound realization - in the ledger of life, sometimes you're the asset, sometimes you're the liability, and sometimes, you're just a footnote in someone else's grand narrative.

But through it all, I never lost my sense of humor. I would occasionally reference the 'ghost class' in future lectures, a twinkle in my eye, a gentle reminder of the day when my love for finance echoed off empty walls, a witty recollection that would bring a knowing smile to those who heard it.

When the Dean, a woman of stern disposition and relentless pursuit of academic excellence, learned of this, her reaction was as volatile as the stock market on a bad day. She summoned me to her office posthaste, her face a canvas of consternation and disbelief.

"Hemant, this is unprecedented!" the Dean exclaimed, her voice echoing off the walls adorned with diplomas and commendations. "A classroom as vacant as a banker's heart during a recession. What do you have to say?"

I adjusted my glasses and offered a grin. "Well, Dean, it seems today the market demand for my class has experienced a temporary bearish trend. But fear not, for every bear market is followed by a bull."

The Dean, unamused, paced the room like a caged tigress. "This is no laughing matter, Hemant! We must devise a strategy to rectify this. Our reputation, our funding – it's all at stake! What according to you, is leading to indiscipline amongst students."

I said, "As I embarked on my traditional teaching methods, I quickly encountered the challenge of maintaining discipline in a classroom of Gen Z students with notably short attention spans.

- The most evident challenge was the omnipresence of digital devices. Students were often more engaged with their phones and laptops than the lecture, leading to a fragmented attention span. I noticed that even the most interested students struggled to stay focused for more than a few minutes at a time.
- The Gen Z students, accustomed to interactive and fast-paced content, found the static nature of traditional lecturing disengaging. This disconnect often manifested in restlessness, side conversations, and a general air of inattentiveness.

- I realized that part of the discipline issue stemmed from a lack of perceived relevance. The students struggled to see how these financial theories applied to their lives and future careers, making it hard for them to invest their attention fully.
- Observing the students, I noted that their attention peaked during brief, interactive segments of the class, such as when they were asked direct questions or presented with real-world scenarios. However, these moments were few and far between in the traditional setup.

As a result of these factors, instances of indiscipline became more frequent. Students would often arrive late, leave early, or engage in parallel activities, creating a challenging environment for both teaching and learning. These observations are pivotal to us. We need to recognize that to teach this new generation effectively, we must adapt our methods to their learning style. This should mark the beginning of my journey toward a more **dynamic, engaging, and humorous approach** to teaching finance, tailored to the unique needs and characteristics of Gen Z learners."

"So, what shall we do?" the Dean pondered.

I leaned forward, my mind already drafting a balance sheet of possibilities. "I propose a solution akin to a strategic investment. Why not capitalize on this opportunity to revamp our approach? Let's introduce real-world scenarios, guest speakers from the finance industry, and maybe even a financial simulation game. We need to diversify our teaching portfolio, so to speak."

The Dean, initially skeptical, slowly nodded, the gears in her mind visibly turning. "A refresh, you say? That might just be the disruptive innovation we need. But will it work, Hemant?"

My smile widened. "In finance, as in education, risk and reward go hand in hand. It's time we invested in the future of our students."

With a newfound sense of purpose, the Dean agreed to the proposal. Over the following weeks, I transformed my course, infusing it with practical experiences and interactive lessons. The word spread like wildfire among the students, and soon, the once-empty classroom brimmed with eager minds.

As the semester progressed, my class became the most talked-about course on campus. Impressed by the turnaround, the Dean couldn't help but express her admiration. "Hemant, you've done it. You've turned a loss into a profit!"

I chuckled, adjusting my glasses again. "Just applying a bit of financial wisdom to education, Dean. After all, in both fields, it's all about knowing when to buy low and teach high".

One of the interesting experiments in this process was out of necessity. Let me recall the same. I suffered from tooth pain and had to book an urgent appointment with my dentist. As I prepped for my impending dental appointment, I found myself in a bit of a crunch. This was similar to when I discovered my wisdom tooth was more rebellious than a bull market on a downward spiral.

My dilemma was not merely the impending battle with the dental drills but finding a replacement to teach my class. I knew that entrusting my class to just anyone would be like letting a novice trader loose on the stock exchange floor – potentially catastrophic.

After much contemplation and a few pain-induced grimaces, I decided on Mr. Prasad, the retired finance professor known for his dry humor that was drier than a balance sheet without liabilities. The students, accustomed to my dynamic lectures, were in for a day of monotone musings about financial prudent, more soporific than wanting to be engaged when you can't.

Before departing, I drafted an email to my students, a masterpiece of finance puns and witty wordplay. "Dear Future Investors," it began, "I'm currently diversifying my portfolio of bodily health and liquidating a troublesome asset (read: wisdom tooth). Mr. Prasad will ensure your intellectual capital continues to accrue interest in my absence. Please extend to him the same attention you'd give a sudden market fluctuation."

The day of the dental reckoning arrived, and as I reclined in the dentist's chair, my thoughts were not on the looming extraction but on whether my students would appreciate the irony of discussing liquidity while I was, quite literally, drooling at the dentist's.

Upon my return, I was greeted with a barrage of emails from my students, each more humorous than the last, detailing Mr. Prasad's lecture, which was surprisingly peppered with unexpected quips about the Great Depression being less depressing than his lecture style.

In the end, students realized that the real investment wasn't in my teachings but in the joy and camaraderie they shared with me. As for my wisdom tooth, it was safely tucked away in an envelope, a tangible dividend from my unexpected day off.

In the hallowed halls of academia, where knowledge reigns supreme and PowerPoint slides flicker like modern-day cave paintings, I, whose experience was as vast as my tie collection, embarked on the journey of applying new teaching techniques.

I'd trained the bright-eyed MBA aspirants of yore back when 'digital disruption' was merely a nuisance caused by an errant finger on a calculator. Now, I faced a new breed of students: the Gen Z BBA warriors, armed with smartphones and a startling ability to create memes at lightning speed.

My teaching philosophy was simple: "If you can't dazzle them with brilliance, baffle them with bull... I mean, business theories." But as I looked out at my new class of 40, who could swipe left on my lectures with the same ease they did on their dating apps, I knew I needed more than just the old-school charm and a well-placed business anecdote.

So, I embarked on a mission: to make learning as addictive as social media and as fun as the videos that kept these youngsters glued to their screens. I was determined to mold these digital natives into business titans, one TikTok reference at a time.

I stood at the helm of my classroom, a sea of Gen Z faces glancing up from behind screens. "Today, we dive into the exhilarating world of finance," I announced, my voice tinged with the excitement usually reserved for unboxing videos. "But fear not, I'll ensure it's more engaging than scrolling through your endless social media feeds."

The class, a blend of mild curiosity and habitual screen-scrolling, looked up. Finance, presented by a professor who seemed to regard the stock market with the same reverence as a viral cat video, was an unexpected twist.

"Let's consider the stock market as the ultimate social network," I began, striding across the room with flair. "Shares are like posts. Some go viral; some barely get any likes. And just like your online reputation, you must manage your portfolio carefully."

The students exchanged amused glances. Finance, explained through the lens of social media? This was something new.

I pressed on, drawing parallels between influencer trends and market fluctuations, likening IPOs to the grand debut of a YouTube star. The room buzzed with interest. I was not just teaching finance but translating it into a language peppered with hashtags and viral vernacular.

As the class neared its end, Sagar raised his hand. "Professor, will we analyze stock trends using TikTok dances next class?" he asked, a playful grin spreading across his face.

I chuckled. "Only if you promise to teach me the moves," I replied, the classroom erupting into laughter.

As the days unfolded, my finance lectures started becoming the talk of the campus. Word spread about a finance class that was less about daunting figures and more about relatable narratives.

I introduced a segment where I analyzed financial trends through popular memes. "Think of 'stonks' memes," I explained one day. "They're simple, funny, and oddly insightful. Much like the stock market, they reflect a bizarre reality."

I developed a class activity where students created hashtags for different investment strategies. "#DiversifyOrDie" and "#RiskItForTheBiscuit" became instant hits among the students, encapsulating complex concepts in catchy, social media-friendly phrases.

I dedicated a lecture to the 'Influencer Economy.' "Influencers are like blue-chip stocks," I quipped. "Highly valued, always in the spotlight, and their worth can plummet with just one bad scandal."

Embracing the challenge head-on, I even started a weekly segment called 'TikTok Trading Time,' where students explained financial concepts through short, engaging TikTok videos. These sessions were not just educational but became a creative outlet, much to everyone's surprise.

Through these innovative approaches, I wasn't just teaching finance; I was revolutionizing it. I turned what was once a dry subject into a vibrant, interactive, and utterly Gen Z-friendly experience. The students began to see finance as a subject and a dynamic and integral part of their digital lives.

With my three decades of corporate escapades, I was a treasure trove of anecdotes, each more amusing and instructive than the last. My journey from the boardroom to the classroom was sprinkled with humorous gems that I shared with my students.

I often regaled my students with tales from the pre-email era, my favorite being 'The Great Fax Fiasco.' It involved sending a crucial financial report via fax, only to realize pages were stuck together, leading to some hilariously misguided business decisions. "And that, my young friends, is why we double-check our digital attachments," I concluded with a wink.

I shared stories of the Y2K panic, where I was part of a team preparing for the 'digital apocalypse' that never happened. "We stocked up on canned food and backup generators, only to welcome the millennium with a whimper, not a bang," I chuckled, comparing it to modern-day viral overreactions.

I had a front-row seat to the dot-com bubble burst, an experience I likened to a roller coaster designed by a madman. "Companies valued at millions without earning a dime – it was like investing in a unicorn farm," I said, my eyes twinkling with the absurdity of it all.

I turned my experience with corporate jargon into a playful segment called 'Jargon Jamboree.' Students would throw out overused business phrases, and I would translate them into plain English, often with a humorous twist. "Synergy? You mean getting along. Paradigm shift? Fancy talk for 'new idea.'"

I introduced the concept of "risk and return" by recounting my ill-fated investment in a yoyo company - "a venture that had its ups and downs, much like my career," I quipped. For the first time that semester, the class erupted into laughter, and even the student perpetually asleep in the back row cracked one eye open.

Then there was the episode with the 'Great Spreadsheet Saga.' Pari, a student more interested in her Instagram feed than Excel formulas, had somehow turned her financial model into a digital abstract art piece. "Bravo, Pari," I applauded, "you've just invented a new form of financial expressionism. Now, if only we could get your numbers to be as creative as your formatting."

But the crowning jewel of my comedic saga was during the final exam review session. Sagar, notorious for asking questions without ever listening to the answers, inquired, "Professor, will the exam cover everything?" Without missing a beat, I responded, "Only everything we've covered, Sagar. I promise there won't be questions on 17th-century Mogul poetry, although the financial stability of King Birla's court is quite an interesting case study."

Through these stories, I didn't just teach finance; I brought it to life with a dash of humor and a pinch of nostalgia. My anecdotes served as a bridge, connecting the dry financial concepts with the real, often absurd, world of business.

It was a sunny Thursday afternoon when I sauntered into the university's grand auditorium for what was billed as a 'Riveting International Guest Lecture' on contemporary economic theories. My skepticism was as high as the national debt, but as a staunch believer in academic camaraderie, I couldn't resist the allure of a gathering of minds as varied as the stock market on a volatile day.

Much like the Sensex on an unpredictable streak, the event started with Professor Linda Bates, a fiery advocate of Keynesian economics. Linda, with the fervor of a Wall Street bull, charged through her presentation, arguing for increased government spending. Her passion was admirable, but her slides, packed with more graphs than a geometry textbook, were as hard to follow as a whisper in a hurricane.

Next up was Professor Richard Thomson, a stoic monetarist, who, in stark contrast, approached the podium like a bear in a bull market. His monotonous tone could make even the most caffeinated student drowsy. Richard's devotion to fiscal restraint was as rigid as his expression. His speech was as predictable as a savings account's interest – safe, steady, but frankly, a bit dull.

Amidst the ensuing coffee break, the murmurs of the crowd were a mix of intrigue and bewilderment, much like my first encounter with cryptocurrency. During this intermission, I bumped into Professor Emily Chang, the unconventional behavioral economist. Emily, always a wildcard, expressed her views with the unpredictability of a day trader. Her anecdotes about irrational investor behavior were as colorful as the stock ticker, yet they left many traditionalists in the room looking as confused as tourists in a foreign stock exchange.

The grand finale was Professor Albert Klein, the esteemed guest speaker known for his eclectic blend of economic theories. Albert's presentation was as diverse as a well-balanced portfolio, touching on everything from classical economics to the latest trends in digital currencies. His charismatic delivery was reminiscent of a savvy CEO delivering a pitch to eager investors. The room was abuzz with energy, though one couldn't be sure whether it was due to the content or the approaching end of the lecture.

As the event concluded and the professors dispersed like traders after the closing bell, I couldn't help but reflect on the rich tapestry of opinions that had unfolded. Much like this gathering, the world of economics was a blend of contrasting theories and personalities, each as vital to the discourse as diversification is to a portfolio.

In the world of academia, just as in finance, it's the varied opinions and spirited debates that drive progress and innovation. As I walked back to my office, I realized that despite our differences, each of us, in our own unique way, contributed to the ever-evolving, wonderfully complex world of economic thought.

I often found that my greatest investment challenge hasn't been in stocks or bonds but in the elusive market of student attention. To attract attention, I had the grand idea to invite a renowned guest lecturer. He wasn't just any Dalal Street wizard; this man could make the Sensex dance tango with his forecasts.

I thought the announcement would send a wave of excitement through my classroom, like a bullish market on a tech stock revelation. Instead, I was met with a collective shrug that could rival the Great Depression's depth of disinterest. Undeterred, I decided to employ every tactic in my academic arsenal.

First, I tried the classic bait – extra credit. This maneuver was as subtle as a corporate takeover and about as successful. A few heads lifted, like stocks, after a minor rally, but the overall market of enthusiasm remained bearish.

Next, I ventured into the dangerous terrain of humor. "He predicts futures better than a crystal ball!" I proclaimed with a flourish. My joke landed about as well as a poorly timed stock buy – a few polite chuckles echoed through the room, akin to the dismal clinking of loose change in an empty piggy bank.

In a final, desperate bid, I played into their tech-savvy hearts. "He's the Elon Musk of Finance!" I declared. This seemed to pique some interest, like a sudden spike in penny stocks. But was it genuine curiosity or just the hope that the guest might resemble the eccentric billionaire?

The day of the lecture arrived, and to my surprise, the hall was packed. Students were perched on every seat, some even standing at the back. Had my marketing ploys worked, or had the word 'free pizza' on the event flyer played a pivotal role? As I looked at the sea of faces, some bright with anticipation, others clearly there for the culinary incentives, I realized my efforts hadn't been in vain.

The guest speaker wove magic through his words, turning complex financial concepts into captivating tales of risk and reward. I watched as the flame of interest was kindled in my students' eyes, their expressions shifting from mild curiosity to rapt attention.

Ultimately, it wasn't just about luring them to a lecture. It was about showing them that finance, much like life, can be unpredictable, thrilling, and profoundly rewarding. As the students filed out, animatedly discussing the lecture, I felt a sense of accomplishment. I had managed to spike their interest, even if it took a little creativity and a lot of pizza.

In the grand ledger of my teaching career, this day would be marked with a bold, green uptick – a small victory in the volatile market of education.

One breezy autumn morning, I encountered a situation far beyond the usual scope of my finance lectures. A student, let's call him Mr. Kesto, stumbled into class, reeking of what could only be described as a distillery's worst nightmare.

Kesto, swaying slightly like a pendulum unsure of its time zone, found his way to a seat in the back row. His arrival was not discreet; it was accompanied by the clatter of books and the rustle of paper, creating a symphony of academic disturbance.

With my sharp gaze that could dissect a balance sheet at thirty paces, I peered over my glasses. "Mr. Kesto," I began, my voice calm yet carrying the subtle edge of authority, "I see you've come to my class under the influence of...spirits. Tell me, are you here to learn about fiscal liquidity or to demonstrate it personally?"

The class erupted in laughter, but my voice had a gentle humor, the kind that teaches rather than chastises.

Kesto, struggling to maintain both his balance and dignity, mumbled something incoherent, sounding vaguely like a drunken merger of apologies and economic theories.

"Ah," I continued, undeterred, "Perhaps you're illustrating the concept of volatile markets. Unpredictable, unstable, and potentially disastrous."

The laughter softened, and in that moment, something remarkable happened. Instead of sending Kesto out, I began to tailor my lecture around the economics of alcohol production, from fermentation processes to market impacts. Kesto, slowly regaining some semblance of sobriety, began to take notes.

By the end of the class, Kesto had not only learned about supply and demand curves in the whiskey market but also about the unpredictable nature of life and choices. As the students filed out, I handed Kesto a water bottle and a brochure for the campus counseling services.

"Mr. Kesto," I said with a kind smile, "Remember, in both finance and life, it's about balance. Losing it can be costly, but regaining it is always valuable."

As Kesto left the classroom, his eyes showed a new understanding. It was a lesson in finance and life, delivered not through stern words but through wit and wisdom. I was picking up the trademarks of a truly great teacher.

As the semester progressed, the unique attributes of each student began to shine brighter, playing a pivotal role in transforming the finance class into a vibrant forum of learning.

Bhanu's Market Analysis Workshops

After class, Bhanu started leading small workshops, applying theoretical concepts to current stock market scenarios. These sessions became popular for their practicality and real-world relevance. Bhanu also created a competitive investment simulation game. Students formed teams to manage virtual investment portfolios, fostering a spirit of competition while learning about risk management and investment strategies.

Leena's Cross-Disciplinary Projects

Leena initiated a project that combined marketing and finance, illustrating the financial implications of marketing campaigns. This project helped her peers appreciate the interconnectedness of business disciplines. She also organized bi-weekly forums discussing international business and its financial implications. These discussions were eye-openers for many, highlighting the global nature of finance.

Arjun's Business Finance Diaries

Arjun shared his experience of managing finances in his online business, giving his classmates insights into entrepreneurial finance. His 'Business Finance Diaries' became a regular feature in my class. Arjun started offering tutorials on financial modeling, simplifying complex concepts for his classmates. His clear and methodical teaching style made these concepts more approachable.

Emma's Fintech Fridays

Emma introduced 'Fintech Fridays,' where she discussed the latest in financial technology. These sessions were eagerly awaited, especially by those interested in tech's role in finance. She also led discussions on behavioral economics, combining her knowledge of psychology with financial principles. Her sessions provided a unique lens through which to view financial decision-making.

Nithin's Practical Banking Insights

Nithin shared anecdotes and lessons from his internship at the bank, giving a practical edge to the theoretical knowledge being taught. His real-world examples made finance more tangible. He started visualizing complex financial concepts through graphic design. His artistic interpretations helped demystify tough topics, making them easier to grasp.

Under my mentorship, these students learned from me and each other, creating a rich learning tapestry woven from their varied experiences and perspectives. This collaborative environment was key in bridging the gap between traditional finance education and the dynamic needs of the modern world.

CHAPTER FOUR

POP QUIZZES AND POP CULTURE: BRIDGING THE GENERATION GAP

I sat at the dinner table; my forehead creased in worry. Around me, the kitchen buzzed with the lively energy of my family. Rani was dishing out her Fish Curry with rice while our daughters, Jui and Jia, debated the latest social media trend.

"I just don't know how to get through to them," I sighed, pushing my glasses up my nose. "This new generation of students seems so... different."

Rani, with a knowing smile, placed a comforting hand on me. "Well, dear, maybe it's time you tried to speak their language."

I raised an eyebrow. "And what language would that be?"

Jui, ever the social media guru, chimed in, "TikTok, obviously. You should totally make a TikTok account, Dad!"

Jia snorted, almost spilling her cold drink. "Yeah, imagine Professor Banerjee doing the latest dance challenge to explain behavioral finance!"

My eyes widened in mock horror. "Dance? I think not. I have a reputation to maintain!"

Rani laughed, "Maybe not dancing, but how about showing your human side? Share stories and be relatable. Gen Z loves authenticity."

"And memes, Dad," Jui added enthusiastically. "You've got to use memes! They're like the universal language of humor now."

Rani nodded in agreement. "She's right. A little humor goes a long way."

I pondered, tapping my chin thoughtfully. "Memes and stories, huh? Perhaps I could start my lectures with a meme that ties into the day's topic. And maybe share a few anecdotes from my college days."

Jia beamed. "See, you're getting it! Gen Z isn't that hard to understand. Just show them you're more than just a professor. Give a Pop Quiz. Show them you're human, too."

As the family continued their meal, the air was filled with laughter and ideas. I felt a spark of inspiration light within me. Maybe teaching Gen Z wouldn't be as daunting as I thought. I was ready to take on the challenge with Pop Quiz.

First, I decided to embrace social media. I created a Twitter (X) account for my class where I posted daily interesting facts related to the course material, accompanied by trending hashtags. To my surprise, the students followed the account and actively participated by retweeting and responding.

Intrigued by the positive response, I delved into interactive technology. I introduced Kahoot quizzes at the end of each lecture, which turned the usually dull Q&A sessions into a lively competition. The students' laughter and cheers when someone got the right answer were music to my ears.

Remembering my daughters' advice, I also tried my hand at gamification. I created a leaderboard in my online class portal, where students earned points for class participation, project submissions, and quiz scores. This seemingly simple addition sparked a friendly rivalry among the students, increasing engagement.

As the clock struck ten, I gazed over my spectacles at the sea of relaxed faces before me. Today, I harbored a secret—a pop quiz, an academic ambush that would soon rattle the tranquility of my unsuspecting audience.

"I have a little surprise for you all," I announced with a mischievous twinkle in my eye, reminiscent of a child unveiling a prank. The classroom, usually a hub of whispered side conversations and surreptitious phone scrolling, fell silent. Even the air seemed to hold its breath.

As I distributed the quizzes, the room transformed into a tableau of emotions. Arjun, the perennial overachiever, lit up like Diwali Lights in July, his pen poised like a knight ready for battle. Beside him, Pari, whose relationship with finance was as tumultuous as a soap opera romance, resembled a deer caught in headlights, her face a canvas of despair.

In the back row, Sagar, a notorious sleeper, jolted awake, his dreams of raising seed capital abruptly replaced by the real-life horror of an unexpected test. His neighbor, Emma, a wizard in calculations but a hermit in class participation, cracked her knuckles, a subtle display of confidence.

As the students dove into the quiz, I leaned back, observing the varying strategies unfolding before me. Bhanu attacked each question with surgical precision; his brow furrowed in concentration. After a few moments of abject panic, Sagar began scribbling what appeared to be a desperate plea to the finance gods.

Meanwhile, Pari's strategy seemed to involve a lot of staring into the void, perhaps hoping the answers would materialize from the ether. On the other hand, Emma worked through the questions quietly, her pen dancing gracefully across the page.

Twenty minutes later, the quizzes were collected, and the atmosphere in the room shifted from acute stress to post-battle exhaustion. With a smile, I reassured them, "This was not just a test of your knowledge but a lesson in preparedness – a key ingredient in the world of finance."

As the students filed out, a buzz of animated conversations erupted. Some debated answers, others shared their shock, but all were united in a newfound respect for the unpredictability of my class.

Ultimately, the surprise quiz was more than a mere assessment; it was a witty reminder that in finance, as in life, one must always expect the unexpected.

I started designing more quizzes with my comic touch. Questions often came with humorous options, making even wrong answers a source of entertainment. "Choose the least terrible option," I'd say, "like picking a movie to watch on a plane."

Through these engaging and amusing methods, I was not just teaching finance but instilling a love for the subject in my students. My class was a place where laughter and learning went hand in hand, transforming the daunting world of finance into an approachable and enjoyable journey.

I introduced a board game I developed called 'Budgetopolis.' In this game, students navigated through various financial challenges, from unexpected expenses to investment opportunities. The twist? Players had to explain their financial decisions in the most humorous way possible. "It's not just about winning," I would say, "it's about laughing at your bankruptcy."

Fridays became known for the 'Stock Market Stand-up' where students presented financial news in a stand-up comedy routine format. From poking fun at bizarre market trends to satirical takes on economic policies, these sessions turned finance into a source of laughter and learning.

I dedicated one monthly class to 'Financial Faux Pas' storytime. Here, I shared real-life financial blunders, both my own and famous ones, analyzing them with a humorous lens. "Remember folks, it's okay to make mistakes, as long as you can find a way to laugh about it later... and learn, of course."

My finance class continued to break the mold, engaging students in projects and presentations that were as educational as they were entertaining.

I assigned a project called 'Finance in Film,' where students analyzed the financial accuracy in popular movies. From the laughable portrayal of trading in "The Wolf of

Wall Street" to the surprisingly on-point depiction in "The Big Short," students presented their findings with a mix of critical analysis and humor. "Remember," I would advise, "Hollywood loves drama more than accuracy, much like Wall Street."

In a nod to the popular TV show, students participated in 'Shark Tank' parody sessions. They pitched ludicrous business ideas with tongue-in-cheek financial plans. Guest faculty members and I played the role of a skeptical investor, often responding with witty retorts and challenging questions, making the exercise a lively and laughter-filled learning experience.

I introduced an 'Economic Stand-up Debate' where students discussed serious economic topics but were encouraged to infuse humor. Topics ranged from the viability of cryptocurrencies to the impact of global trade wars, all presented in a light-hearted yet informative manner. This not only enhanced their understanding but also their ability to communicate complex ideas simply.

Students were asked to keep a 'Personal Finance Diary,' tracking their spending, savings, and investing habits. At the end of the month, they shared their experiences, often revealing amusing and enlightening financial mishaps and learning. I used these diaries to discuss personal finance management in a relatable and engaging way.

Through these innovative assignments, I created a classroom environment where finance was no longer a dreaded subject but an exciting field to explore. My students were not just learning about finance; they were experiencing it in an informative and enjoyable way.

As the semester progressed, the impact of my unique approach to teaching finance became increasingly evident through student feedback and their learning outcomes.

I regularly held informal feedback sessions, humorously dubbed 'Roast or Toast.' Here, students openly shared their thoughts on the class. Most students expressed how the fun atmosphere made the daunting world of finance approachable and engaging. "It's the first time I've laughed in a finance class without it being due to confusion," Leena quipped.

There was a notable increase in class participation. Students who were initially hesitant to speak up began eagerly contributing, often with clever remarks or insightful questions. The humorous environment fostered a sense of comfort and encouraged open communication and debate.

My playful yet informative teaching methods led to a deeper understanding of financial concepts. Students could easily discuss complex topics like derivatives, market dynamics, and investment strategies, often using the analogies and humorous examples I introduced in class.

The creativity and quality of student projects were significant indicators of their enhanced learning. Whether it was through parody pitches, film analyses, or economic debates, students demonstrated a clear grasp of financial principles, often applying them in innovative ways.

The enjoyable learning atmosphere resulted in better grades and a genuine interest in finance. Students began exploring financial news, markets, and trends outside the classroom, a testament to my success in making finance relevant and exciting for them.

Through my unorthodox yet effective teaching style, I transformed my finance class into a hub of laughter, learning, and practical understanding. My students were not just prepared for exams; they were equipped with a real-world understanding of finance, all thanks to making learning fun.

Each student brought their unique perspective, creating a rich tapestry of interactions and discussions.

Bhanu often contributed by relating financial theories to real stock market trends, offering analytical insights during discussions, which added depth to the class debates. His ambition drove him to excel, often challenging his classmates to think critically about investment strategies and personal finance management. Bhanu often linked finance with technology, sparking conversations about fintech and blockchain, which added a modern twist to the class discussions.

Pari bridged the gap between marketing and finance, often illustrating how financial decisions impact marketing strategies, making her contributions invaluable for practical understanding. With her interest in international business, she frequently brought up global economic issues, enriching class discussions with a broader perspective

As an entrepreneur, Emma shared real-life experiences of managing finances in business, providing practical examples that resonated with her peers. Her strength in financial modeling and her methodical approach helped demystify complex financial concepts, making them more accessible to her classmates.

Leena's understanding of psychology allowed her to offer unique perspectives on consumer behavior and financial decision-making, enriching class debates. Working part-time at a bank, Leena shared practical insights into everyday financial operations, providing a glimpse into the practical aspects of finance.

Sagar's artistic background led him to approach finance creatively, often visualizing financial concepts uniquely, which added an artistic flavor to the discussions.

These diverse perspectives not only enlivened the classroom but also helped bridge the gap between traditional financial education and the multifaceted world of modern finance. Under my guidance, the students began to see finance not as a standalone subject but as an interconnected part of a larger world.

Another unique feature was the makeup quiz, where the students were greeted not by a piece of paper but by a monopoly board. "Today, you will play Monopoly," I declared. "But not just any Monopoly – Financial Crisis Monopoly!"

The rules were bizarre. Passing 'Go' deducted money, Chance cards were replaced with 'Stock Market Crash' cards, and the 'Free Parking' space was now 'Tax Audit.' The game was chaos. Leena landed on 'Tax Audit' three times in a row, while Arjun kept getting 'Stock Market Crash' cards, forcing him to mutter about bear markets and his impending doom.

In a twist of fate, it was Pari, the coffee-saving entrepreneur, who triumphed, not by mastering finance but by hoarding every property she landed on, a strategy she proudly called 'The Caffeine Monopoly.'

After the game, I announced, "Congratulations! You've just learned the most important lesson in finance – expect the unexpected."

The students left the class not just with a grade but with a newfound appreciation for the unpredictability of finance. And me? I was already plotting the next quiz – something about chess and international economics.

On another fateful day, I strutted into class with a grin wide enough to rival the Sensex on a good day. "Class," I announced, twirling my marker like a cowboy's revolver, "Today, we're diversifying our portfolio of knowledge with a surprise quiz!"

Groans echoed off the walls, sounding like the stock market crash of '92. But I was undeterred. "And," I added with a mischievous twinkle in my eye, "it's not just any quiz. It's a real-life simulation!"

The students exchanged nervous glances. Emma, an aspiring hedge fund manager, whispered to her neighbor, "Does this mean we're getting real money?" Her neighbor, Arjun, who was more interested in corporate ethics, shrugged. "Maybe he'll make us calculate the moral depreciation of our souls."

I cleared my throat, silencing the room. "You will each receive an envelope. Inside, you'll find your starting capital – Monopoly money – and a series of challenges. Your task: maximize your wealth by the end of the class. The top three earners get an A; the rest try not to declare bankruptcy."

The class erupted into a chaotic trading floor. Emma immediately started short-selling properties she didn't own. On the other hand, Arjun set up a 'corporate ethics consultancy' booth, charging five Monopoly dollars for moral advice.

Halfway through the class, I threw in a twist. "Breaking news: there's a housing market crash in the world of

Monopoly!" I bellowed. Emma's empire crumbled, forcing her to mortgage her imaginary properties.

As the clock ticked down, the students were frantic. Then, just as the bell was about to ring, I announced, "Stop trading! Now, let's reflect on what we've learned."

The students, now exhausted tycoons, looked around at the Monopoly money littering the floor. I beamed at them. "Finance isn't just about making money; it's about strategy, risk, and sometimes, sheer luck. But remember, the real value lies in the experience, not just the numbers on a spreadsheet."

As the students filed out, still a bit dazed, Emma turned to Arjun. "Maybe there's more to finance than just profit." Arjun nodded, pocketing his 'corporate ethics' earnings. "And maybe there's more to ethics than just lectures."

I watched them leave, a satisfied smile on my face. The quiz crisis was more than just a test; it was a lesson they'd never forget.

Once, during this semester, I found myself in a peculiar conundrum. My department, once a bustling hub of number crunchers and market wizards, was now as desolate as a Wall Street trading floor on Christmas Day. With resignation waves hitting harder than a stock market crash, my colleagues and I faced a daunting task: convincing Dean Monjolika, a woman as immovable as a fixed asset, to recruit additional faculty. It was impacting our ability to take quizzes as we were taking additional classes.

The scene unfolded in the dean's office, a room so austere it could double as a vault. Armed with spreadsheets and graphs, I presented my case with the passion of a bullish investor during a market rally. I was joined by Professor Adams, an econometrics wizard, and Professor Sam Bonds, whose jokes about the bond market were the stuff of legend. We formed a trio that was not unlike the fluctuating patterns of a volatile market.

"Dean," I began, my voice steady like a long-term investment, "our department is facing an unprecedented deficit in human capital. Without reinforcement, we risk depreciating our educational value."

Dean Monjolika, peering over her bifocals with the skepticism of an auditor, remained unmoved. "And how do you propose we finance this expansion? Magic beans?"

Professor Adams chimed in, "Well if we had magic beans, we'd diversify them across different asset classes."

Even Dean Monjolika cracked a smile, albeit a brief one.

Professor Bonds leaned forward, adding, "And I assure you, Dean, the return on investment in faculty will be much higher than my last joke."

Amidst the laughter, I outlined the benefits of a diversified faculty portfolio, promising innovative courses and research that could attract grants and donations like blue-chip stocks.

As the meeting drew to a close, the air was charged with anticipation. Had we swayed the dean's fiscal conservatism into a bullish stance on recruitment?

Finally, Dean Monjolika sighed, her expression softening. "Alright, I'll consider your proposal. But remember, I want returns on this investment – no junk bonds or speculative ventures."

We exited the office, feeling cautiously optimistic. In the world of academia, just like in finance, the risk was inherent, but so were the prospects of great rewards. Our spirits lifted, much like the markets on a good day. We had planted the seeds for a future flourishing with academic prosperity, or at least, that was the investment we hoped for.

Next week, we faculty members were embroiled in an amusing yet thought-provoking battle. It was a fight not against market forces or economic theories but against the most daunting adversary known to academia: **the request to teach additional credits.**

The story began on a sunny afternoon when our dean, a woman who considered every problem solvable by adding more work to her faculty, convened a meeting. With the glee of a child in a candy store, she announced that due to budget cuts and an unexpected decrease in faculty, everyone needed to teach extra credits. The news spread across the room like a bad stock tip during a market crash.

I, known for my love for leisurely afternoons pondering over economic models, almost choked on my coffee. Beside me, the Professor, an expert in obscure tax laws, looked like someone had proposed abolishing the Income Tax Act. Meanwhile, a young, enthusiastic professor whose theories often crashed more spectacularly than the '29 stock market seemed the only one excited by the challenge.

As the dean droned on about "institutional synergy" and "leveraging intellectual assets," I whispered that I have a plan to my colleagues. We met in the faculty lounge, where all the faculty members looked at me expectedly. I leaned back in my chair and exclaimed, "I've got it! The perfect plan to ensure our courses remain empty!"

The Tax Expert raised an eyebrow, skepticism clear in his voice. "Oh? And what might that be, Hemant?"

"We'll devise courses so ludicrous, so incredibly niche, that no student would dare enroll," I said with a sly grin.

Professor Adam chuckled, "You mean like 'The Economics of Underwater Basket Weaving'?"

"Exactly! But even more absurd. I'm thinking 'Financial Implications of Left-Handedness,'" I replied, my eyes twinkling with mischief.

The professors, who usually couldn't agree on whether Keynes or Friedman had the better mustache, united in an act of academic insurrection.

Later, as the classes surprisingly filled up, we, the professors, met again.

"I don't understand," I groaned, "They were supposed to be deterrents!!!"

Professor Nirma leaned against the doorframe, a smirk on her lips. "Well, Hemant, it seems we've underestimated the curiosity of our students. Or perhaps we've underestimated the appeal of the unusual. My 'Coin Toss Predictability in Consumer Decision Making' class is now standing room only."

I sighed, "I'm swamped with papers on left-handed CFOs. What have we done?"

Professor Mamta laughed, "It looks like we've made learning fascinating again, my friends."

As we adjusted to our newfound popularity in the following weeks, I asked rhetorically, "So, what unique challenges do left-handed CFOs face in a right-handed world?"

A student shouted from the back, "Ergonomic challenges with right-handed desks!"

The class erupted in laughter, and even I couldn't help but chuckle. "Excellent point. And what about biases in decision-making processes?"

The next day, students arrived in my "Advanced Hedge Fund Strategies" class to find it transformed into "Hedge Fund Strategies for Wizards," a course blending finance with fantasy. "Taxation 101" became "The History of Tax Evasion in Pirate Societies." I, embracing the chaos, simply replaced my "Introduction to Investments" with "Investing in Mars Colonies: A Practical Guide."

The students, initially baffled, soon embraced the whimsy. Who wouldn't want to learn about offshore banking from Captain Jack Sparrow or explore the financial implications of wizarding currencies?

The dean, however, was less than thrilled. Her face, upon sitting in my lecture on the investment strategies of Hogwarts, was akin to an investor who had mistakenly shorted Apple stock before a product launch.

In the end, the dean had to relent. She couldn't fire her entire department and secretly admired our creativity. The faculty returned to their regular teaching loads, but the legend of our resistance lived on, much like a well-invested endowment, providing returns of laughter and inspiration for future semesters.

In the midst of the dynamic changes and interactive learning environment, I noticed that a small group of students remained disengaged and uninvolved in class activities. Addressing this became a crucial part of the transformation.

I scheduled one-on-one meetings with these students to understand their perspectives and challenges. I realized that factors like personal learning styles, external pressures, and lack of confidence contributed to their disengagement.

Based on these meetings, I introduced more varied teaching methods to cater to different learning styles. I incorporated more infographics and videos for visual learners, and for kinesthetic learners, I incorporated more hands-on activities and simulations.

A peer mentorship program was established, pairing less engaged students with actively participating students. This program provided additional support and a comfortable space for them to express themselves and get involved.

I restructured some class sessions into smaller discussion groups, making them less intimidating and more conducive for shy or reticent students to participate.

I introduced reflective journals as a part of the coursework, allowing students to express their thoughts and ideas in writing, which was particularly beneficial for those who were less comfortable speaking in front of the class.

I continued to assign projects that required students to apply financial concepts to real-world scenarios relevant to their interests. This approach helped make the subject matter more relatable and engaging for all students.

I consistently encouraged feedback and suggestions from all students, ensuring that the less engaged students' voices were heard and their ideas considered in shaping the class.

I emphasized the importance of a supportive and non-judgmental classroom culture where every student felt valued and motivated to participate.

Through these efforts, I gradually engaged the previously disengaged students, ensuring that the transformed learning environment was inclusive and beneficial for every student in my class.

CHAPTER FIVE

POWERPOINTS AND POINTLESS ARGUMENTS: A TYPICAL TUESDAY

It was the first day of another new semester, and this Tuesday, I embarked on my inaugural academic quest. Now, navigating the labyrinthine corridors of the Business School Building was no small feat. It resembled less a place of higher learning and more a particularly sadistic level in a video game designed by architects with a fondness for M.C. Escher, the Dutch graphic artist. After a series of wrong turns, a close encounter with a broom closet masquerading as a seminar room, and an impromptu tour of the ladies restroom, I finally located Classroom G - a room so cunningly hidden that one might suspect it was witness protection.

Breathless but triumphant, I entered the classroom, where I was greeted by the expectant faces of a few of my students. The room, equipped with what could only be described as a control panel suitable for launching spacecraft, presented its next challenge. The smartboard, an impressive slab of technology that promised interactive learning, stood before me like a monolith.

Undeterred, I approached the smartboard with the same determination I applied to my research on Behavioral Finance. However, my attempts to coax life into the electronic behemoth were met with stubborn resistance. Taps, swipes, and even the occasional pleading stare failed to yield any results. It was as though the smartboard was a cat that had decided not to acknowledge my existence.

Not to be outdone by a mere piece of technology, I attempted to awaken the sleeping audio system, which quickly became an auditory adventure. The speakers, having lain dormant all summer, decided to greet the new semester with a symphony of feedback screeches, much to the students' amusement.

Realizing that I was quickly losing my audience to an unintended comedy show, I did what any self-respecting academic would do in a crisis. I called for reinforcements from the IT department. With a swift intervention from a young tech wizard, who performed what seemed like digital alchemy, the smartboard sprang to life, and the audio system began to purr like a well-fed cat.

Given the earlier theatrics, the rest of the lecture went smoothly or as smoothly as expected. Undaunted by my initial technological misadventures, I delivered a captivating lecture on finance principles, occasionally punctuated by the smartboard flickering in solidarity.

As the students filed out at the end of the lecture, one lingered behind to offer a piece of advice, "Professor, next time, try turning it off and on again. Works every time." With a newfound respect for both the wisdom of my students and the quirks of university technology, I made a mental note to enroll in a workshop titled 'The Mysteries of the Modern Classroom: A Survival Guide.'

Thus concluded the first day of the new semester in my academic life, a day marked by humility, learning, and a gentle reminder that sometimes, the biggest challenges in academia aren't found in the complexities of finance but in the simple task of getting the smartboard to cooperate.

The morning sun peeked through the blinds, casting long, lazy shadows across the cluttered desk of mine. It was another Tuesday, a day notoriously packed with lectures, meetings, and the never-ending battle with my PowerPoint slides, which seemed to possess a mind of their own.

I yawned, stretching my arms above my head, and glanced at my watch. 7:30 AM. Perfect. Enough time to tweak my lecture on fiscal policies before the pandemonium of breakfast with my family.

I shuffled to the kitchen, where chaos reigned supreme. With an uncanny ability to solve complex equations and yet burn toast consistently, Rani was in the midst of her morning routine.

"Morning," I mumbled, reaching for the coffee.

"Don't you dare touch that mug! That's mine," Rani said without looking up from her half-burned toast. "You can wait two minutes for the next batch."

I rolled my eyes but obediently waited. Our daughters, Jui and Jia, were bickering over the last bit of cereal. Jui, the ever-dramatic 23-year-old, proclaimed the injustice of sharing a bathroom and cereal with her 19-year-old sister.

"Dad, tell Jia to stop taking all the Chocos!"

"Girls, it's too early for World War III over cereals. Share," I interjected, finally grabbing my cup of coffee.

Jia smirked. "And you're going to convince your students about the importance of the economics of sharing today?"

"Economics is rational. Teenagers, not so much," I retorted.

After surviving breakfast, I hurried back to my fortress of solitude (otherwise known as my home office) to finalize my PowerPoint. Today's topic: The Intricacies of Financial Markets. Riveting stuff. I could already picture the sea of half-asleep students.

Halfway through my slides, my computer decided it was a perfect moment to crash. "Not today," I groaned, frantically trying to reboot it.

Rani popped her head in. "Everything okay?"

"My PowerPoint just crashed. I have a lecture in an hour!"

"Did you try turning it off and on again?"

I shot her a look. "Very funny."

Somehow, I managed to resurrect the presentation. I glanced at the clock. 8:45 AM. Time to leave.

At the university, my day was a blur of lectures, student queries, and back-to-back meetings. My PowerPoint, despite its earlier rebellion, behaved impeccably.

Returning home, I found Rani and the girls in the kitchen, embroiled in what appeared to be a heated debate over the merits of pineapple on pizza.

"Pineapple does not belong on pizza!" Rani declared.

"It's a fruit, Mom. It's healthy!" argued Jia.

I sighed. Another typical Tuesday. I wondered if there were any Chocos left.

I stood before my 'Intro to Finance' class, squinting at the PowerPoint presentation projected behind me. My slides, a chaotic mix of Comic Sans and Times New Roman, were as much a staple of my lectures as my mismatched socks.

"As you can see," I said, pointing to a graph that looked more like abstract art than financial analysis, "the economic trends are clear as mud."

In the third row, a student whispered, "Does he mean clear or muddy?"

It was a typical Tuesday in my life. Post-lecture, I ambled to the staff lounge, where the coffee was as bitter as the ongoing debate about the department's budget.

"Ah, Hemant, still using those prehistoric PowerPoint templates?" chided Dr. Adam, his nose buried in a graph-filled magazine.

"Better ancient than inaccurate," I retorted, recalling Adam's infamous forecasting blunder last semester.

I proceed for my lunch. Lunchtime was a theatrical display of my multitasking ineptitude – a Paratha in one hand, grading papers with the other, occasionally mixing up the two. My comments on student essays were often speckled with mustard stains, much to the confusion and amusement of my students.

The afternoon also brought the dreaded Faculty Meeting. As the Dean droned on, my thoughts wandered to my evening plans – a thrilling rendezvous with my latest financial thriller novel.

My phone buzzed just as the meeting threatened to become an eternal trap. A text message from my favorite niece: "Uncle H, remember you promised to teach me about stocks tonight!"

Ah, real life. Far more unpredictable than any market trend. I excused myself, mumbling something about urgent research.

As I left, I heard Dr. Adam's voice, "Probably off to adjust his PowerPoint animations."

Little did they know, my Tuesday was about to become an enlightening adventure in explaining short selling to a ten-year-old.

That Tuesday, I never knew my day was about to take a turn from the academic to the absurd. My idea of a wild day was rearranging my bookshelf by the color of the spines, and I was about to be thrust into the whirlwind world of administration.

The Dean, with a penchant for dramatic pauses, had summoned me to her office. The room was as grandiose as the Dean's personality, adorned with an array of trophies celebrating academic achievements and a suspiciously high number of 'World's Best Dean' mugs.

"Prof Hemant," the Dean began, her voice rumbling like distant thunder, "I have a special assignment for you." My heart skipped a beat, visions of prestigious research projects dancing in my head. "I'm entrusting you with administrative responsibilities."

The words hit me like a poorly-constructed pie chart. Administrative responsibilities? Me, a man who considered filling out a tax form akin to an extreme sport. The Dean continued, blissfully unaware of my internal turmoil, outlining duties that included budget management, committee meetings, and – horror of horrors – organizing the annual faculty retreat.

As I embarked on this unexpected journey, my days were filled with a comedy of errors. Budget spreadsheets became my arch-nemesis, each cell taunting me with a maze of numbers. Committee meetings were an exercise in patience as I navigated the delicate egos of my colleagues. And the faculty retreat? Let's just say that choosing a 'Survivor' theme was not my best idea.

Now, for me, 'administrative responsibilities' were akin to having an alien life form thrust upon me. I was more at home deciphering Keynesian theories' mysteries than the cryptic language of administrative forms.

On my first day as an administrator, I entered my new office – a stark contrast to my cozy, chaotic academic den. I was greeted by a mountain of paperwork, each sheet whispering tales of budgets, schedules, and something terrifyingly titled 'strategic planning'. I looked around helplessly, feeling like a fish trying to climb a tree or, more aptly, an economist trying to navigate bureaucracy.

My first task was scheduling. It seemed simple enough until I realized it was akin to solving a Rubik's cube blindfolded. Every change I made pleased one and infuriated three. I soon found that in the jungle of academia, 'scheduling' was the lion, and I, unfortunately, was not equipped to be the lion tamer.

Then came the budget meetings, where numbers danced before my eyes, not in the elegant waltz of economic theories but in a frenetic, incomprehensible tango. Terms like 'fiscal sustainability' were thrown around, making me long for the comforting complexities of the Laffer Curve.

Despite these challenges, I persevered with a spirit that would have made Bahubali proud. I discovered that hidden beneath the jargon and paperwork were opportunities to make a real impact. I found novel ways to funnel resources into research, championed innovative teaching methods, and even streamlined some of the dreaded bureaucratic processes.

Through it all, my sense of humor never waned. I regaled my students with tales of my administrative adventures, each story more outlandish than the last. My lectures, once a bastion of economic theories, now included anecdotes about the perils of paper jams and the diplomacy required to handle coffee machine disputes.

Ultimately, I emerged from my stint in administration with a newfound appreciation for the unsung heroes of academia – the administrators. I returned to my research with a spring in my step, a twinkle in my eye, and a secret stash of 'World's Best Professor' mugs, just in case the Dean ever needed a gift idea.

As the clock struck three on the first Tuesday of the month, I, a seasoned veteran in the battlefield of finance, armored myself with a steaming cup of coffee, bracing for the imminent siege known as the monthly faculty meeting. I often mused that if time truly was money, these gatherings were the epitome of fiscal irresponsibility.

The meeting room, a dreary chamber adorned with charts and diagrams akin to hieroglyphics for the uninitiated, was abuzz with a cacophony of academic fervor. I often likened these assemblies to a stock market floor, where ideas were traded, sometimes too hastily, and the value of patience was grossly underestimated.

First on the agenda was the budget review, a topic that made my ears perk up like a broker hearing a stock tip. However, the discussion quickly devolved into a debate over trivial expenditures. I chuckled to myself, noting the irony in finance professors struggling to balance a budget; it was like chefs debating over how to boil water.

Then came the committee updates, a parade of progress reports that moved with the urgency of a glacier in no particular hurry. My mind wandered to the fluctuating markets, pondering if my stocks were having a better afternoon than me.

The pinnacle of the meeting arrived unannounced – the suggestion to revamp the curriculum. Eager voices rose, each professor an advocate of their own specialty. I threw in my two cents, proposing a course on "The Economics of Faculty Meetings." The room erupted in laughter, a rare currency in these gatherings.

As the hands of the clock marched onward, I reflected on the paradox of my profession. Here I was, a connoisseur of efficiency, a maestro of maximizing returns, yet bound by the bureaucratic symphony that played the same tune every meeting.

I often found myself in the midst of these most paradoxically amusing yet frustrating experiences known to academia – faculty meetings. These gatherings are less like well-oiled machines and more akin to a carousel of eccentric characters, each more colorful than the last, spinning in an orbit of opinions and peculiarities.

The first character who springs to mind is Professor Nirma, a marketing genius with a memory like a steel trap rusted shut. Her recollections of past meetings are a patchwork quilt of misremembered resolutions and fantasized protocol. She often reminisces about discussions that never happened and decisions that were never made, leaving the rest of us wondering if we'd slipped into an alternate universe.

Then there's Professor Mamta from the Psychology department, who seems to have an affinity for diversity over individuality, or colleagues, for that matter. She often drifts into lengthy monologues about her latest research on the Psychology of Diversity, while we, the captive audience, are diverse about empathy and patience. Her green hypothesis may be commendable, but it's the green light on decisions we often miss in her lengthy psychological digressions.

Let's not forget Professor Rambling – oh, sorry, I meant Ramsey – from the English department. His eloquence is only matched by his inability to reach a point. His speeches, peppered with Shakespearean quotes and obscure literary references, are like a labyrinth with no exit. One cannot help but admire the journey, though you often forget where you started and still have no idea where you're going.

In contrast, Professor Gupta from Mathematics is all about brevity. His contributions to discussions are like mathematical equations – short, precise, and often leaving the rest of us struggling to catch up. His responses are binary; it's either a firm "yes" or a definitive "no," with no room for the grey areas that the rest of us inhabit.

As a Professor of Finance, I spend time calculating the odds of a productive outcome, investing my time in what often feels like a stock market of opinions – volatile, unpredictable, and occasionally rewarding. These meetings, though maddening, are a fascinating study of characters, a place where diverse minds collide, creating a kaleidoscope of perspectives.

As the gavel hits the wood, signaling the end of another meeting, I can't help but smile at the absurdity of it all. In the ledger of my academic life, these meetings are entries I would never dare to balance – their value lies in their sheer unpredictability and the colorful human element that no balance sheet could ever capture.

As every meeting gets adjourned with a sigh of relief, I gather my papers, thoughts, and unspent quips, saving them for the next adventure in faculty meetings. The world of finance was unpredictable, but the comedy of faculty meetings was a guaranteed return.

As the clock struck three in the hallowed halls of our venerable institution of higher learning, an issue of monumental importance arose: the selection of the High Tea menu for the upcoming guest faculty lecture in the faculty meeting. Our mission was singular yet critical - to entice our dear students to attend a guest lecture on finance, a topic they often find as dry as unbuttered toast.

The committee, a motley crew of academicians, gathered in the conference room, a battlefield where the aroma of dry-erased markers clashed with the lingering scent of stale coffee. Today, I was at the helm; my reputation in finance was only eclipsed by my notorious indecisiveness about lunch menus.

"I propose Samosa!" declared I, with the confidence of a man who had never faced the wrath of a horde of hungry undergraduates. "Simple, elegant, classic!"

"Elegant? My dear Hemant, this isn't Majestic Bus Station at Bengaluru! We need pizzazz, something to really draw in the crowds," retorted Dr. Nirma, a marketing guru who believed all of life's problems could be solved with the right branding strategy.

"Bagels and cream cheese," mumbled Professor Adam from behind his mountainous pile of economic research papers. "It's a crowd-pleaser."

The debate raged on, with suggestions flying like arrows in a medieval skirmish. Wada Pav, Dahi Wada, Butter Masala Dosa - the ideas were as diverse as the faculty's publication records.

Meanwhile, I lost in a sea of contemplation, stroked my chin thoughtfully. My mind wasn't on pastries or finger sandwiches but on the intricate dance of supply and demand curves, wondering if there was a correlation between the elasticity of baked goods and student attendance.

Just as the clock inched agonizingly towards the hour, a stroke of genius hit me. "What if," I started, the room falling silent, "we serve a variety of options but also include something unexpected, like... mini–stuffed Idlis?"

The room erupted in a chorus of agreement, a rarity in academia. Mini-stuffed Idlis were the perfect metaphor for finance - seemingly straightforward but filled with complexities and surprising elements.

And so, the menu was set. The day of the lecture arrived, and to the surprise of many, the room was packed. Students chattered excitedly, plates piled high with an assortment of High Tea delights. We may never know whether it was the Mini Stuffed Idlis or the allure of financial knowledge, but I smiled contentedly, a man at peace with my decision - at least until the next faculty meeting.

CHAPTER SIX

THE GREAT GRADING DEBACLE: RED PENS AND REDEMPTION

Once upon a time, a peculiar tradition existed within my household in the tranquil suburb of Bengaluru. The tradition was known as the Great Grading, a comical series of events that unfurled every semester end, involving me, my sharp-witted wife Rani, and our two astute daughters, Jui and Jia.

The Great Grading commenced when armed with a battalion of red pens; I would barricade myself in my study to grade the mountainous stacks of finance exams. The air would buzz with the fervor of scholarly judgment, occasionally punctuated by my exasperated sighs and the relentless scribbling of red ink.

Outside the study, Rani and the girls would commence their humorous observations. "Look, the red ink reservoir is depleting faster than the stock market in '08!" Jui remarked, peering through the keyhole with the expertise of a seasoned spy.

"Shh, I believe he's about to perform his ceremonial 'F for effort,'" Jia would add as they listened to the rhythmic tapping of the pen like analysts predicting market trends.

Rani, always the voice of reason, yet with a mischievous twinkle in her eye, would prepare 'redemption snacks' – treats designed to soothe the soul after a long day of academic judgment. "Chocolate for the As, nuts for the Bs, and for the Cs... well, let's hope the man likes biscuits," she would jest as the girls giggled in anticipation.

But the true humor lay in the aftermath. Post-grading, I would emerge, looking as if I'd just negotiated a difficult merger. My family would be waiting, armed with their observations and cheeky commentary. "Ah, the wielder of the red pen returns! How fares the market of academic futures?" Rani asked, her eyes dancing with mirth.

As the evening wore on, we would all sit together, sharing stories and laughter, the tension of grading dissipating like a bear market turning bullish. In these moments, I realized the true value lay not in grades but in the love and light-heartedness of my family. The Great Grading was not just a quirky tradition but a reminder of the joy and humor that could be found in the every day, even amidst red pens and redemption.

I was also notorious for my unyielding grading style. My red pen, feared by many, was rumored to contain ink made from the tears of undergraduates.

One day, as spring blossoms began to invade the campus, a grading debacle of epic proportions unfolded. It all started when I decided to revolutionize my grading system. "Why use percentages," I mused, "when I can grade them based on the current stock market values?" Thus, students' grades fluctuated wildly with the SENSEX, causing both euphoria and despair in equal measure.

Meanwhile, Sagar watched in horror as grades soared and plummeted. Sagar secretly harbored dreams of stand-up comedy and decided it was time for some lighthearted intervention. He swapped my dreaded red pen for a glittery pink one infused with sparkles and a faint bubblegum scent.

The next batch of graded papers caused quite a stir. Students were initially puzzled and then burst into laughter upon receiving their essays, now adorned with comments like "Stellar Analysis!" and "This needs more liquidity – and by liquidity, I mean clearer arguments! " written in shimmering pink.

This unexpected twist led to an unforeseen turn in my persona. Embracing the change, I began incorporating humor into my lectures. Phrases like "Let's dive into the liquidity pool of knowledge!" and "This topic is more volatile than Bitcoin on a bad day!" became commonplace. My lectures, once dreaded, became the most attended, with students eager for a dose of finance with a side of fun.

In response to a question about short-term liquidity, one student wrote, "It's like my relationship status – it's complicated, but it can be managed with proper commitment." I chuckled, awarding points for creativity if not accuracy.

Another, asked to explain the concept of risk and return, said, "It's like asking someone out. You risk embarrassment for the potential return of a date." As I sipped my coffee, I wondered if perhaps we should include a chapter on romantic risk management.

In a question about depreciating assets, a student compared it to their car, a "venerable old beast that loses value every time my dog decides it's a moving chew toy." Imagery and finance, I noted, made strange but amusing bedfellows.

But the pièce de résistance was an essay on ethical finance. One student, weaving a narrative around an imaginary company, crafted a tale of intrigue, embezzlement, and redemption that would put a soap opera to shame. It was clear: here was a finance student with the soul of a novelist.

I found unexpected creativity in that pile of papers, among calculations and analyses. As I graded, I realized that these students, with their unique insights and humor, were not just learning finance; they were learning to think, question, and express themselves.

One answer on a paper read, "Inflation is when money starts social distancing from its real value." I chuckled, my eyebrows arching in amusement. "Ah, the wit of youth," I murmured, awarding points for creativity if not accuracy.

Another student had illustrated the concept of 'supply and demand' with a sketch of a desert island where the only 'supply' was a vending machine, and the 'demand' was a line of cartoonish, desperate castaways. I laughed out loud, the sound echoing in the solemnity of my study. "Economics meets art," I noted, scribbling a bonus point for artistic effort.

Amidst the heap of papers, I found one that defined 'market volatility' as "what happens when Dalal Street has too much coffee." I snorted in laughter, my usual stoic demeanor giving way to a rare display of mirth. "Coffee does seem to fuel more than just morning routines," I jotted in the margins.

As I perused the final exam, my eyebrows arched in amused surprise. Question one asked for a definition of 'liquid assets', and young Miss Jenkins responded, "Anything you can quickly convert into cash or cocktails, preferably the latter." I chuckled, making a mental note to remind the class that while humor was appreciated, the stock market was less forgiving than me.

The next paper, belonging to Leena, contained a diagram of the economic cycle that more closely resembled a rollercoaster at Wonderla than any textbook illustration. I smirked, thinking how fitting it was, given the recent market volatility. "Accurate, if not academic," I scribbled in the margins.

As the hours ticked by, I encountered answers ranging from hilariously absurd to ingeniously insightful. One student had reimagined 'bull and bear markets' as an actual bull and bear in a boxing ring, duking it out over stock prices. Another had penned a haiku about fiscal policy, surprisingly profound in its brevity.

Finally, as the clock struck midnight, I leaned back in my chair, a satisfied smile playing on my lips. The papers were graded, but more importantly, I had been reminded of the vibrant creativity that often lay hidden beneath the serious veneer of finance. "Economists of the future, perhaps not. But certainly, philosophers and artists," I thought.

The climax of this grading debacle occurred during finals. I, now dubbed "Professor Pink Pen" by my students, announced that the final exam would be a live, improvised comedy show where students had to present their financial knowledge humorously. The event was a resounding success, with students creatively intertwining economic concepts with witty punchlines.

In the end, I learned the power of humor in education, and the students learned that even in the serious world of finance, there's always room for a good laugh. As for Sagar, he realized that sometimes, the best way to solve a problem is with a touch of creativity and a pink pen.

Another interesting episode in grading again involved my red pen while being in the faculty lounge. The Great Grading Debacle unfolded in the dimly lit faculty lounge, where the aroma of strong coffee perpetually lingered as an insistent advisor. It was an ordinary Thursday, or so it seemed, until my red pen, a notorious instrument of academic judgment, ran dry.

"What ho!" I exclaimed, my mustache quivering with the intensity of a Shakespearean tragedy. "My red pen has surrendered to the void!"

Dr. Mamta, a psychology professor with a penchant for melodrama, peered over her half-moon glasses. "A sign, perhaps, that your relentless critique of the passive voice has finally exhausted the ink."

Laughter echoed, bouncing off the walls lined with books that had witnessed many such debates.

Enter Dr. Adam, the idealistic Economics professor. "Why not try a green pen? Research shows it's less intimidating for students."

The suggestion hovered in the air like a daring plot twist in a freshman's first short story.

Mamta scoffed. "Green is for gardening, not grammar!"

Meanwhile, Professor Nirma, the enigmatic marketing teacher, sipped her espresso, her eyes twinkling with unspoken tales of syntactic adventures. "In Banaras, we grade with whatever color inspires us. Sometimes, it is blue like the melancholy of Kabir's poetry."

Professor Gupta, the stoic math professor, chimed in with a rare smile. "I once tried grading in invisible ink. It was quite effective until the students realized they had to hold their papers near a heat source to view their marks."

The room erupted with laughter, a welcome interlude in the otherwise monotonous task of grading.

"The Great Grading Debacle," as it came to be known, taught the faculty members an invaluable lesson: sometimes, redemption lies not in the color of the pen but in the educator's heart. And perhaps, just perhaps, in a little dash of humor.

My finance classroom, notorious for my love of red pens and aversion to grade inflation, had turned into a miniature battlefield one day. As the students filed in, the tension was thicker than the Financial Accounting textbook, which served as an excellent shield for Pari when she saw her grade.

"Ah, the great grading debacle begins," muttered Bhanu, his eyes wide with a mix of fear and anticipation. He flipped his paper over. "B-," it read. He sighed in relief - this was as good as an A in my world.

Pari peeked through her fingers at her paper, her face morphing into an expression that was a cross between seeing a ghost and winning the lottery. "C+? I am the chosen one!" she exclaimed, holding her paper like a victorious flag.

Next to her, Sagar stared at his paper as if it were written in ancient hieroglyphics. "D for 'delightfully adequate'?" he mused. "At least he didn't use the red pen to draw a sad face this time."

In the corner, Arjun, the class topper, held his paper with trembling hands. A minus sign next to his A seemed to glare at him like a tiny, inked monster. "The horror," he whispered, his dreams of a perfect GPA slipping away like sand through fingers.

I, meanwhile, leaned back in my chair, observing the chaos with a smirk. My red pen, a feared weapon of mass deduction, lay on the table, its cap off, almost as if it were taunting the students.

As the initial shock wore off, the students gathered in small groups, sharing their "war stories." Laughter and groans filled the room as they compared their red-inked battle scars.

Sagar clapped Bhanu on the back. "At least we survived the Red Pen Massacre of 2024."

"True," Bhanu replied, "but I think the real test will be explaining this to my parents."

The bell rang, signaling the end of the period, but the story of the Great Grading Debacle would live on, a humorous tale of red pens and redemption in the annals of finance class history.

In the hallowed halls of Pathsala University, where tradition often clashed with technology, there was an unwritten rule, more sacred than the formulae inscribed in ancient textbooks – 'Thou shalt not use thy Smartphone in Professor Banerjee's finance class.' It wasn't just a preference; it was almost a doctrine.

I treated calculators with the reverence most reserved for religious artifacts and believed these gadgets were the only true companions for my budding financiers. "A calculator," I would often say with a twinkle in my eye, "is a financier's Excalibur!"

During one fateful morning, the great' Calculator Revolt' took place as the autumn leaves waltzed to the ground outside. The students, armed with the latest Smartphones, staged a silent protest. The screens of their devices lit up with financial formulas and stock market apps, were like tiny beacons of modern rebellion.

I entered the class with my usual brisk enthusiasm and stopped dead in my tracks. My eyes, hidden behind thick glasses, widened at the sight. It was as if I had walked into a scene from a futuristic movie where calculators had become extinct.

The tension in the air was thicker than the economics textbooks gathering dust on the shelves. I adjusted my glasses and spoke with a sigh that seemed to carry the weight of bygone eras. "I see the digital age has finally infiltrated my sanctuary. But let me tell you something, dear pupils, there's something about punching numbers into a calculator - it's like feeling the heartbeat of finance!"

There was a moment of silence before the room erupted into laughter. Even the most tech-savvy students couldn't resist the charm of my wit. That day, they learned a valuable lesson, not just about finance, but about the importance of respecting the old while embracing the new.

From that day on, Smartphones were used less frequently, not out of fear, but out of respect for a professor who could outwit technology with humor and wisdom. In my own quirky way, I had taught them that sometimes, the best way to deal with change is not to resist it outright but to adapt with grace and a touch of humor.

But this rule again got broken in a month's time. I was pacing the examination hall like a hawk surveying its territory. The room was filled with the sound of pencils scratching and the occasional cough, a symphony of academic endeavor.

Suddenly, my sharp eyes caught a flicker of light from under a desk. Jake, the class's notorious procrastinator, was trying to conceal his mobile phone. I ambled over with the nonchalance of a seasoned detective.

"Ah, Mr. Jake," I said, my voice dripping with irony, "it appears you've mistaken this examination for a phone-a-friend trivia challenge."

The class, caught between anxiety and the absurdity of the moment, struggled to stifle their laughter.

"I was just checking the time, Professor," Jake mumbled, his face the color of the Economics textbook he'd barely opened.

"Checking the time, you say? In my class, we adhere to the old-fashioned method of timekeeping. It involves looking at the clock on the wall, not scrolling through stock market updates."

My wit was not lost on the class. They knew my reputation for using humor to teach complex concepts, like using the principle of 'opportunity cost' to explain why studying was better than partying.

"Let me offer you a quick lesson in risk versus reward, Mr. Jake," I continued, now addressing the entire class. "The risk you took by using your phone was expulsion, a rather high cost for the reward of Googling Keynesian economics? I would've hoped our discussions on rational decision-making would've sunk in by now."

The room erupted in quiet giggles. My ability to turn a situation into a teachable moment was legendary.

"But, in the spirit of educational growth and because I detest paperwork, your punishment will be different. You, Mr. Jake, will present a lecture next week on the ethical implications of cheating in academia and its effects on market trust. Think of it as your contribution to the economic education of your peers."

As I walked away, the class couldn't help but admire the ingeniousness of my approach. Not only had I addressed the issue with humor, but I had also turned it into a learning experience for everyone.

Jake, now known as the 'reluctant lecturer,' learned more about ethics and economics in preparing that presentation than he ever would have by scrolling through his phone. And I, with my witty and educational response, had once again proven why I was a favorite among the students.

As a Finance Professor at Pathsala University, I've seen my fair share of bizarre occurrences, but nothing quite compares to this spring semester of 2021. If there's one thing I've learned, it's that numbers may not lie, but students certainly have a penchant for creative fiction.

Firstly, there's Sagar. Sagar arrived with a calculator the size of a small car, insisting it was necessary for "optimal financial computations." By week three, he was using it as a lunch tray. His method of depreciating the value of his sandwiches was quite innovative.

Then we had Pari. Pari decided to relate every financial concept to her cat's behavior. Bonds were compared to her cat's loyalty, while market volatility was akin to its mood swings. Her presentation on "Feline Fiscal Policies" was as enlightening as it was absurd.

But the crown jewel of eccentricity was undoubtedly Riya. Riya, a believer in the supernatural influence on economics, would perform a séance before every major exam, trying to channel the spirit of Adam Smith for guidance. The janitor was the only spirit she ever seemed to summon, wondering why there were candles in the classroom.

Despite these antics, there was a certain charm to their enthusiasm. Sagar's calculator became a class mascot of sorts. Pari's feline analogies, while odd, actually helped some students better grasp the concepts. And Riya's séances, though unsuccessful in reaching the afterlife, did bring about a sense of camaraderie among the students.

In the world of finance, where unpredictability is the only certainty, perhaps a touch of the unconventional isn't so out of place. After all, isn't the market itself a tapestry woven from diverse, often irrational human behaviors?

So, as I close the ledger on another semester, I can't help but smile at the thought of these future financial experts. They may not always follow the conventional path, but they've certainly added some color to the black-and-white world of finance. And for that, I'm surprisingly grateful.

In the hallowed halls of finance academia, where the scent of money is as intoxicating as the promise of power, let me share my most challenging conundrum this time. It wasn't the stock market's enigma or the labyrinth of derivatives but the case of the twin test-takers, Azaad and Shazaad.

On a crisp autumn morning, as leaves painted the campus in shades of gold and amber, my midterm exam in Advanced Financial Strategies unfolded with the usual suspects – furrowed brows and frantic scribbling. But amidst the cerebral orchestra, two notes played in suspicious harmony: the Kapoor brothers, as identical in their test-taking strategies as they were in visage.

During the last hour of the exam, I spotted it – a mirrored ballet of wandering eyes and synchronized pen strokes. They copied from each other with such artistry that I almost applauded – almost. Their not-so-clandestine exchange was more blatant than insider trading at a company picnic.

Post-exam, in my office lined with books that smelled of wisdom and dust, I summoned the duo. They entered, aghast and as synchronized in their steps as they were in their academic duplicity.

"Azaad, Shazaad," I began, my tone a mix of disappointment and wry amusement, "your performance today was...remarkable. An impeccable demonstration of tandem thinking. Do you apply the same collaborative effort in understanding derivatives as you do in replicating each other's answers?"

Their faces, mirrors of mortification, suggested they hadn't anticipated getting caught. I continued, "In finance, we value original analysis, not echoing another's investment strategy. Or, in your case, answers."

I paused, watching them squirm. "However, given your evident talent in mirroring each other, I'm offering you a choice. Redo the exam separately, in different rooms, or accept a joint venture into my new course, 'Ethics in Finance.'"

The twins exchanged a glance, a silent conversation that I was sure involved less economic theory and more survival strategy.

They chose the redo. On their way out, I added, "Gentlemen, remember, in finance and life, the most profitable investments are integrity and hard work. There are no shortcuts to genuine success."

As they left my office, their sheepish nods were the first dividends of a lesson I hoped would be compounded with interest in their careers.

And so, in a world where wealth is often amassed through shrewd tactics, I found a small victory in teaching two promising minds the value of honesty. After all, in the stock market of life, integrity is the currency with the highest returns.

Office Hours and Existential Crises: The Student Parade

The bell tolls the end of another finance lecture at Pathsala University, signaling not just the close of an academic sermon but the commencement of the great student parade. With a PhD in Finance and a minor in Sarcasm, I watched as my pupils shuffled out, heads brimming with theories about supply and demand, their minds far from grasping life's real supply and demand.

My office hours are an open invitation to a circus of existential crises, each student a unique act. First in line is Emma, a bright-eyed sophomore convinced that failing to understand the Laffer Curve will lead to misery and underachievement. I assure her that while understanding fiscal policy is useful, the curve in her social life is what really needs attention.

Next, there's Nithin, a student with a hairstyle as unruly as his financial theories. He's on the brink of creating a new economic model that could either win him a Nobel Prize or earn him a lifetime ban from the Finance department. I encouraged him to aim for the Nobel but to keep the department's number on speed dial, just in case.

In comes Arjun, the overachiever. He's juggling four internships, three research projects, and a paralyzing fear that he's just not doing enough. I remind him that in the ledger of life, balancing work with rest is key, and sometimes, the best investment is a good night's sleep.

As the parade continues, I reflect on my own journey. I once thought money was the currency of success, but months of teaching have given me a different perspective. Success, I now believe, is measured in the moments you impact others, not in the zeros in your bank account.

I always found office hours at the university an entertaining, if not slightly absurd, affair. The steady stream of students resembled a parade of existential crises; each uniquely garbed in their personal blend of confusion and ambition.

One afternoon, as I sipped my filter coffee, I shared my observations with my colleague, Dr. Adam, an economics professor with an equal appreciation for the humor found in academia.

"You see, Adam," I began, adjusting my spectacles, "each student that knocks on that door is a living embodiment of a philosophical conundrum."

Dr. Adam, leaning against the doorframe, raised an eyebrow. "Do elaborate, my friend."

"Well, take Leena, for instance," I said, referring to a bright-eyed sophomore. "She came in here, armed with spreadsheets, asking whether to pursue a career in finance or follow her passion for art. It's the classic head versus heart battle, playing out in real-time."

"And what sage advice did you offer?" Adam inquired, a smirk playing on his lips.

"I told her life's too short for bad coffee and unfulfilling careers. Who knows if she'll take it to heart."

Our conversation was interrupted by a timid knock. A lanky young man with a bewildered look entered. "Professor Hemant, I... um, I have a question about the stock market simulation assignment."

I leaned back, a twinkle in my eye. "Ah, the simulation, where every student gets a taste of omnipotence only to be humbled by the market's invisible hand. What's your crisis?"

The student shuffled his feet. "Well, sir, I invested everything in fintech because, well, fintech is cool... but now I'm virtually bankrupt."

Adam burst into laughter. "Fintech, Hemant! Maybe we should include them in the curriculum."

I, suppressing a chuckle, offered some advice on diversification and risk management while thinking how this mishap was a perfect metaphor for life's unpredictable nature.

As the day waned, we, the professors, reflected on the myriad dilemmas and aspirations we encountered. "You know, Adam," I mused, "despite the absurdity of everything, there's a certain beauty in this parade. Each student, a story, a question, a crossroads."

Adam nodded in agreement. "Indeed, and in guiding them, perhaps we navigate our own existential crossroads."

With that, we closed our office doors, the echoes of shared laughter mingling with the silent wisdom of the empty corridors.

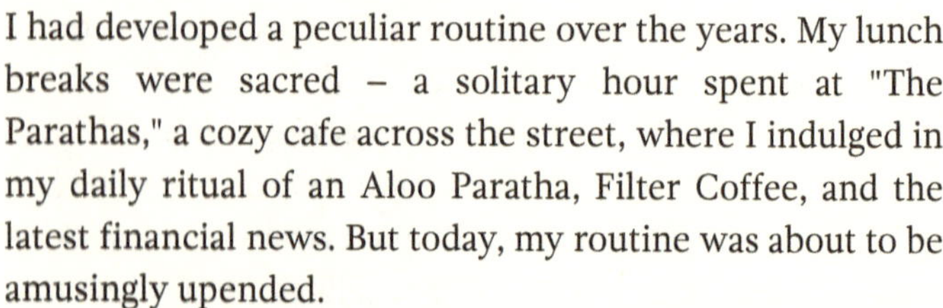

I had developed a peculiar routine over the years. My lunch breaks were sacred – a solitary hour spent at "The Parathas," a cozy cafe across the street, where I indulged in my daily ritual of an Aloo Paratha, Filter Coffee, and the latest financial news. But today, my routine was about to be amusingly upended.

A timid knock echoed through my office as I packed my briefcase with the day's lecture notes. Glancing at my watch, I sighed, realizing my Aloo Paratha would have to wait. In came Emma, a bright but perpetually anxious student, clutching a spreadsheet like a life raft.

"I just don't understand these derivatives," she stammered, spreading sheets of calculations across my desk. As I began to explain, more knocks followed, each signaling another student, another question, another bite out of my lunch break.

The office transformed into a bustling hub of existential crises over GPAs and futures in finance. Amidst explaining bond valuations and equity markets, I couldn't help but smile at the parade of students. Each one carried the weight of the world in their backpacks, yet there was almost comedic desperation in their eyes, as if the mysteries of finance held the key to the meaning of life itself.

Amidst this chaotic symphony of academic angst, my stomach grumbled audibly. Pari, a student known for her blunt honesty, pointed out the obvious. "Professor Banerjee, did you miss lunch again?" The room erupted in laughter, breaking the tension like a well-timed punchline.

As the final student left, I glanced at the clock. My sacred lunch hour was long gone, yet I couldn't suppress a chuckle. "Existential crises and finance," I mused, "a combination as complex and unpredictable as the stock market."

I grabbed my briefcase, deciding to grab a late Paratha, my mind swirling with the humorous absurdity of my missed lunch break. The Cafe would be closing soon, but somehow, that Aloo Paratha seemed less important now. In its place, a warm sense of fulfilment lingered, a reminder that sometimes the most memorable moments are those that disrupt our well-laid plans.

The next day, in the hallowed halls of Pathsala University, the clock struck two, signaling the beginning of my dreaded office hours. These were not ordinary office hours; they were a weekly existential parade where students masqueraded their panic over grades and job prospects with thinly veiled philosophical quandaries.

Today, I had another weight on my shoulders: a memo from Dean Monjolika, crisply typed and stern in tone, instructing me to "reign in the chaos" of my office hours. The Dean, a woman who treated the English language with the precision of a tax audit, had a knack for making simple requests sound like royal decrees.

As the first student entered, a young man with a perpetual frown etched between his brows, I braced myself.

"Professor, I've been contemplating the existential implications of corporate finance. Do you think Nietzsche would have approved of leveraged buyouts?"

I, who had spent most of my morning deciphering the new tax code, found myself momentarily speechless. "Well," I ventured, "Nietzsche did advocate embracing one's will to power. In a way, leveraged buyouts could be seen as a corporate expression of that."

The student nodded solemnly, seemingly satisfied, and shuffled out, only to be replaced by a young woman with hair the color of a traffic cone.

"Professor, if time is a flat circle, as you said in a lecture, does that mean our investments should also be cyclical? Like, should I be investing in sundials or something?"

Suppressing a chuckle, I explained the metaphorical nature of time in financial theories while wondering how Dean Monjolika would react to a sundial investment strategy.

The parade continued: existential crises disguised as questions on balance sheets, the human condition explored through market fluctuations, and somewhere in the midst of it all, I found myself actually enjoying the absurdity.

As the clock hand inched towards four, the last student, a quiet young man with a thoughtful expression, asked, "Professor, do you think our pursuit of wealth is just a distraction from the inevitable void?"

I paused, looking at the young faces that had paraded through my office, each grappling with their own quiet battles under the guise of academic inquiry. With a smile, I replied, "Perhaps, but it's a distraction that teaches us much about ourselves and the world. And sometimes, that's all we can ask for."

As the student left, I glanced at the Dean's memo, now coffee-stained and slightly crumpled. I penned a quick reply: "Chaos somewhat reigned in. Also, might consider investment in sundials. Regards, Hemant."

Since I often found my office hours transforming into a parade of existential crises, a scenario far from the simple Q&A sessions I had initially envisioned, Rani and our two daughters had become my unofficial advisory board on managing these weekly spectacles.

As I prepared for another Tuesday of student consultations, I recalled Rani's recent advice: "Remember, dear, you're not just teaching finance; you're shaping young minds!" I mused that shaping minds was a bit ambitious, considering I struggled to shape my cricket bat swing.

The first student, Sagar, entered with a dramatic sigh. "Professor, I've been contemplating the futility of wealth accumulation in a transient world," he declared.

"Ah," I said, shifting in my chair. "Have you considered diversifying your existential portfolio?"

Jui's advice echoed in my mind: "Dad, sometimes you need to listen more than solve." I nodded sympathetically, letting Sagar unravel his philosophical dilemmas while mentally reviewing the day's stock market trends.

Jia's strategy was all about distraction. "Dad, if they start questioning the meaning of life, ask them about their weekend plans. Works every time."

Sure enough, when Emma, an overachiever with a panic penchant, began to question the ethical implications of capitalist structures, I interjected, "Speaking of structures, how was that architectural boat tour you mentioned?"

Emma paused; her anxiety temporarily rerouted. "Oh, it was fascinating! The guide explained..."

I smiled, grateful for the respite, though slightly guilty for steering her away from deeper waters.

As the parade continued, I reflected on my family's advice. Rani advocated for empathy, Jui for listening, and Jia for distraction. I realized the art of managing my office hours lay in balancing these approaches, blending finance with philosophy and stock advice with life advice.

The last student of the day, Bhanu, summed it up perfectly: "Professor, I don't know if I should invest in stocks or my own mental health."

"Well, Bhanu," I replied, a twinkle in my eye, "why not a bit of both?"

CHAPTER EIGHT

CASE STUDIES AND COFFEE SPILLS: ADVENTURES IN TEACHING

As a seasoned Professor of Finance, the realm of numbers and spreadsheets has long been my sanctuary. But, as fate would have it, an invitation to serve as a guest faculty member at a top B-School would add an unexpected chapter to my academic journey, one rich with humor and self-discovery.

The prospect of teaching bright, ambitious minds was exhilarating, yet daunting. I envisioned classrooms echoing with the clatter of calculators and the rustle of The Wall Street Journal. However, reality penned a different story.

On Day One, I entered the classroom armed with graphs and charts, only to be met with a sea of faces more interested in their social media feeds than the fluctuating stock market. Ah, the challenge had begun. My traditional lectures, it seemed, were as engaging as watching paint dry. I needed a new strategy.

Thus began my foray into the world of humor. I started weaving finance concepts with everyday life, drawing parallels between budgeting and dieting ("You overspend, you have to account for it, just like those extra slices of pizza on your waistline") or explaining complex financial models with dating analogies (ever tried explaining bond yields through the lens of Tinder swipes?).

Surprisingly, the students responded. Eyes lit up, not from smartphone screens, but from understanding. Laughter became common, and not just at my attempts to navigate the college's coffee machine.

I learned to embrace the unexpected. When a student asked if 'liquidity' was a new kind of smoothie, we had a class discussion on clear communication instead of a lecture on financial jargon. When a debate erupted over whether Batman was a better investor than Iron Man, we explored the concept of risk management through superhero finances.

But it wasn't just finance where learning happened. These students taught me about the latest trends, from TikTok dances to what on earth a 'VSCO girl' was. I even attempted a viral dance challenge, leading to much amusement (and a few bruised shins).

Once, as I waxed eloquently about the intricate dance of supply and demand, a hand shot up, belonging to a young woman in the third row. Her name, I recall, was Emily – Emily, with eyes that twinkled with the mirth of unasked questions. At that moment, I fancied myself, Socrates, ready to shape the minds of tomorrow with my profound insights.

"Professor," she began, her voice laced with a curious blend of innocence and mischief, "If inflation is the bane of purchasing power, could we not simply live in a world without money? Perhaps bartering could make a comeback. I'll trade my psychology notes for your finance expertise!"

The room, pregnant with anticipation, suddenly erupted into laughter. My brain, a seasoned machine well-oiled with complex financial models and theories, sputtered and stalled. Bartering? The very foundation of my life's work was playfully tossed aside for a system as ancient as civilization itself.

I stood there, gobsmacked, the ghost of Adam Smith probably chuckling in his grave. The silence was deafening, save for the sound of my incredulity bouncing off my ego's walls. It was then that I realized finance, with all its numbers and graphs, couldn't account for the simplicity of human ingenuity.

So, I did what any self-respecting professor would do. I laughed along, tipping my imaginary hat to Emily. "Well," I conceded, "I suppose I could start accepting apple pies as payment for financial advice!"

The class ended with a round of applause, not for the wisdom of financial expertise but for the lesson in humility served to me on a silver platter by a student's wit. As I packed up my things, still slightly dazed, I couldn't help but marvel at the beauty of teaching – a field where even the teacher, steeped in knowledge, can be the student.

In another class, a simple question from a student left me floundering like a fish out of water.

The incident occurred during a particularly riveting lecture on the intricacies of derivative markets. With my usual flair, I was elucidating the subtleties of financial instruments when a hand shot up from the sea of eager, young faces. The hand owner was a student known for her sharp wit and sharp intellect.

"Professor Hemant," she began, with a twinkle in her eye that should have served as a warning, "if you were to explain the concept of a 'derivative' to a five-year-old, how would you do it?"

The classroom, sensing the shift in the atmosphere, fell silent. Eyes darted between the questioner and me, anticipating a response filled with my usual blend of academic rigor and charismatic eloquence. But to everyone's surprise, my mouth opened and closed, resembling more a gasping guppy than the seasoned lecturer I was.

In all my years of delving into complex financial theories and equations, I never considered how to distill such a concept to its simplest form. The sophisticated frameworks and terminologies I was so accustomed to wielding were useless here. It was as if the student had asked me to explain the color blue to a blind man.

The moment stretched on, with my brow furrowing in thought. Initially tense, the class began to titter, then chuckle, as they realized that their infallible professor had been momentarily speechless.

Finally, with a self-deprecating smile, I conceded, "Well, Sarah, I suppose I'd tell the five-year-old that a derivative is like... when you trade your apple for a promise of two apples tomorrow. Based on a guess, it's trading something you have now for something you hope to have later."

The class erupted in laughter and applause, not out of mockery but in appreciation of the humility and simplicity shown by their esteemed professor. I, though initially stumped, had demonstrated a key lesson that day – that true understanding of a subject is not just in mastering its complexities but also in appreciating its essence in the simplest of terms.

From that day on, I often began my lectures with a reminder: "Remember, if you can't explain it simply, you don't understand it well enough." And in the corridors of the Business School, the student was hailed as the student who had taught the teacher, albeit with a touch of unwitting wit.

As the semester drew to a close, I realized this stint was more than just a teaching assignment. It was a lesson in adaptability, finding humor amidst the serious, and connecting with a generation I once struggled to understand.

As I delivered my final lecture, I glanced at my students - my unwitting teachers - and knew that while I had hopefully imparted some financial wisdom, they had given me something far more valuable: a refreshed perspective and a ledger full of humorous memories.

My life revolved around two things: complex case studies and my undying love for coffee. My hair had seen more winters than a Siberian fir tree, had a reputation amongst the students. Students whispered my name in the corridors with a mixture of awe and fear - awe for my financial wizardry, and fear for my coffee-induced unpredictable lectures.

I, a traditionalist at heart, refused to succumb to the digital age totally. I believed in the power of chalk and blackboard. However, my chalk pieces had a peculiar habit of disappearing. One day, in the middle of illustrating the complexities of hedge funds, I reached for my chalk, only to find it gone. A thorough search ensued, leading to the discovery of a chalk black market among the students, where my chalk was prized for its "wisdom-infused" dust.

In an unexpected twist, I decided to embrace technology and teach a class on Excel for financial modelling. It was a sight to behold – me, squinting at the screen, mistaking the mouse for a remote, and Excel formulas behaving like rebellious teenagers. The class ended with a newfound appreciation for the simplicity of chalk and blackboards.

As finals approached, the students braced themselves. I spoke of the bell curve like a mythical creature, elusive and mysterious. When the grades were released, rumours abounded that I used a complex algorithm involving my coffee consumption patterns to determine the curve. Whether fact or fiction, the grades were always fair, albeit a bit caffeinated.

I, with my coffee stains and chalk-dusted suits, taught more than just finance. I taught resilience in the face of coffee catastrophes, innovation when resources disappear, adaptability in an ever-changing world, and the courage to face mythical curves. I was more than a professor; I was a legend brewed in the depths of finance and filtered through life's many adventures.

One particularly bright Monday, I entered my classroom with my usual air of distracted genius, juggling a stack of papers that held my latest case study, "The Fluctuating Fortunes of Fizzy Pop Inc." On my other hand, I precariously balanced a mug of steaming coffee, a dangerous dance I had yet to master.

As I greeted my class with a scholarly "Good morning," the mug, seemingly with a mind of its own, leapt from my grasp. In what felt like slow motion, the coffee embarked on an aerial journey, baptizing the front row with a spray of caffeine and narrowly missing Arjun, the ever-eager student who always sat upfront, notebook ready, like a knight awaiting orders.

The class erupted into a mixture of gasps and stifled giggles. I, ever the professional, merely adjusted my glasses and quipped, "That, dear students, was a practical demonstration of market volatility and liquid assets." The laughter that followed broke the ice, and even Arjun smiled, his notebook now speckled with a few drops of my brew.

From that day forth, my class became the most popular in the finance department. Rumors spread about my unorthodox teaching methods - was it an accident or a brilliantly crafted teaching tool? Whispers of "coffee spill economics" echoed through the corridors, and students started attending my lectures armed with mugs of their own, just in case learning required a more immersive experience.

Amidst the chaos of case studies and coffee spills, I taught my students more than just finance. I taught them the art of turning mistakes into lessons, of finding humor in mishaps, and the importance of a good dry cleaner. My classes blended theory and the unexpected, much like a good cup of coffee - best enjoyed with a dash of unpredictability.

And so, my legend continued one coffee spill at a time.

After the hectic classes, I sauntered into the faculty lounge with a stack of case studies teetering in my arms. The lounge, a hodgepodge of eclectic furniture and coffee stains, was the unofficial meeting ground for the intellectual and the caffeine-dependent.

"Good morning, esteemed penny-pinchers and stock market whisperers!" I greeted, my voice dripping with a sarcasm only a finance professor could muster.

Dr. Adam, an economics professor with a penchant for colorful metaphors, looked up from his triple-shot espresso. "Ah, Hemant, how's the world of numbers and nightmares?"

"Thriving, as always," I replied, setting my precarious stack on a table. Unfortunately, I didn't notice the open cap of Dr. Gupta's coffee thermos lying in wait. Like a squadron of lemmings, the case studies took a nosedive, bathing in an ocean of lukewarm coffee.

"Oh, the irony!" Dr. Gupta exclaimed. "A finance professor, victim to a liquid asset!"

I, unfazed, simply picked up the top soggy case study. "It seems we'll have a real-world lesson on risk management today." This was one of the most important quotes I've heard in my classes.

I grabbed a handful of napkins, mopping up the mess with the enthusiasm of a bullish market on the rise. "Well," I declared optimistically, "this will add a whole new flavor to the discussion in today's seminar!"

Meanwhile, Professor Nirma, the marketing guru with a flair for the dramatic, chimed in. "Or a lesson in why we need waterproof documents. Market that, Hemant, and you'll be the hero of faculty lounges everywhere!"

As I began rescuing my notes, Dr. Mamta leaned in. "You know, this could be a great case study itself. 'The Great Coffee Spill of 2024: An Exercise in Crisis Management and Resource Allocation'."

Chuckling, I nodded. "And how to keep your cool when your world's awash in coffee. Essential skills for any finance major."

Dr. Adam, the risk-averse professor, gasped in horror. "Hemant, your coffee's ROI just plummeted!" he exclaimed, assessing the damage with a look of dismay typically reserved for unformatted spreadsheets. Dr. Adam, ever the pragmatist, also suggested putting a lid on future coffee cups. He proposed a toast to my unbreakable spirit with his own safely secured cup of tea.

Meanwhile, Professor Gupta, the statistics expert, was already calculating the probability of a repeat incident. "Given the frequency of your coffee consumption and your expressive hand gestures, I'd say there's a 78.3% chance of this happening again before midterms."

As the laughter subsided, they each settled into their chairs, sipping their coffees and discussing their upcoming lectures. The finance professor's case studies, now coffee-stained and a bit crumpled, sat on the table, a silent reminder of the morning's escapade. And at that moment, amidst the aroma of coffee and the camaraderie of my colleagues, the lounge felt less like a simple break room and more like a little haven of academia, spills, and all.

I had a ritual every Sunday morning. Armed with a stack of case studies and a pot of freshly brewed coffee, I'd settle at the kitchen table, prepared for a peaceful morning of work. However, this Sunday was different.

As I opened my first case study, Rani sashayed into the kitchen with an air of determination. "Hemant, it's high time you teach these girls about finances. They think credit cards are just magic money cards!" she pointed toward our daughters, Jui and Jia, who were more interested in their smartphones than fiscal responsibility.

I, ever the educator, saw an opportunity. I cleared my throat, adjusted my glasses, and began, "Well, girls, let me explain the concept of risk and return using this fascinating case study about a multinational corporation—"

I was interrupted by Jia. "Dad, is this going to be like your story about compound interest and the ice cream truck?" she asked with a smirk.

Jui chimed in, "Yeah, or the time you explained mortgage-backed securities using our Monopoly game?"

Rani chuckled, pouring herself a cup of coffee. "Give your father a chance, girls. Maybe today's lecture will be more... engaging."

I, undeterred, launched into my explanation. However, every attempt to delve into the complexities of finance was met with playful banter. When I discussed assets and liabilities, Jui quipped about the "liability" of her sister borrowing her clothes without asking. Discussing investment portfolios led to a debate over whether investing in a new phone case was a wise decision.

As the morning progressed, the case studies remained largely untouched, but the coffee pot emptied, and the kitchen filled with laughter. I, though slightly exasperated, couldn't help but join in the fun, realizing that some lessons were better taught through life itself.

Ultimately, no groundbreaking financial insights were shared that morning, but our family did share something more valuable: quality time and a few good laughs. And perhaps, just perhaps, the girls learned a bit more about finance than they'd admit.

In the evening, I decided to attempt to educate our daughters again. I have always regarded my household as a small, unlisted family company, where my two daughters were budding assets, and my wife, Rani, was the efficient, albeit underappreciated, Chief Operating Officer.

I decided it was the perfect time for a practical lesson. "You see, girls," I began, adjusting my glasses, "understanding finance is crucial. It's all about strategic investment."

From the kitchen, Rani shouted, "And don't forget about the high risk of investing in your dad's hair-brained schemes!"

The girls, Jui and Jia, exchanged a look that said, "Here we go again." Jia, ever the sarcastic one, chimed in, "Dad, is this going to be about stocks, or are we branching out to bonds? Because, you know, I have a very busy schedule of not caring about either."

I, undeterred, continued. "Imagine our family as a company. I am the CEO; your mother is the CFO..."

"More like CEO of Cleaning, Organizing, and Everything Else," mumbled Jui, sipping her milk.

"Yes, well," I faltered, "and you girls are like stocks. You have great potential to appreciate in value over time."

After entering with a tray of coffee and toast, Rani quipped, "And you, dear, are like a depreciating asset. Especially after you try to fix the plumbing yourself."

Ignoring the chuckle from Jui, I pressed on. "Let's discuss diversification. Jui, instead of spending your allowance all on makeup..."

"You mean investing in personal growth and confidence building," Jui retorted with a grin.

"And Jia, those video games are hardly assets."

"Actually, they're teaching me valuable life skills, like how to survive a zombie apocalypse," Jia added without missing a beat.

I sighed, my lesson veering off course like a poorly advised hedge fund. "The point is, managing finances is essential, and..."

Rani cut in, "Speaking of managing, did you manage to remember our anniversary is next week?"

A moment of silence fell. I, the man who could calculate complex algorithms in my sleep, had forgotten the most important date in my personal ledger.

"Ah, well, that is... I had planned to... um, diversify our celebrations this year," I stammered, face reddening faster than a crashing stock market.

The girls burst into laughter, and even Rani couldn't help but smile at my flustered state. "It's okay," she said, patting my hand.

"I've already taken the liberty of investing in a weekend getaway. You can thank me by not talking about finance for two whole days." I said weakly.

As our family finished their dinner, I realized that maybe, just maybe, there were more valuable things in life than dividends and Rupee signs. And at that moment, I couldn't have been more bullish about my family.

Monday after, I found myself in the lavishly oak-paneled office of Dean Monjolika, a woman so stern she could make a statue squirm. My relationship with Dean Monjolika, a woman as strict with university policies as she was with her perfectly coiffed hair, was a blend of respectful antagonism and mutual admiration. We had navigated through countless academic quandaries together, sometimes as allies, often as friendly foes.

"I need a week off, Dean. For a family vacation," I began, as casually as one might comment on the weather.

"A vacation?" Dean Monjolika peered over her spectacles, her eyebrows arching like the peaks of an incredulous mountain range. "In the middle of the semester?"

"Ah, but consider the educational value!" I leaned forward, my hands theatrically spread. "I plan to teach my children the intricate art of bartering in Moroccan souks. It's a practical extension of my Finance 101 class."

Dean Monjolika was unmoved. "Your idea of bartering doesn't include leaving your class in the lurch."

I, never one to be deterred, flashed a grin. "I've arranged for Professor Adam to cover my lectures. He's thrilled at the prospect of escaping his own Economics 201 for a week."

"Thrilled or coerced?" The dean's skepticism was as thick as her leather-bound ledgers.

"Let's call it 'enthusiastically persuaded'," I quipped. "Besides, it's all in the spirit of academic collaboration."

Dean Monjolika sighed, her gaze fixed on a paperweight that seemed less weighty than this conversation. "And what about your Tuesday seminar? The one where you famously demonstrate market fluctuations using monopoly money and dramatic flair?"

My smile didn't falter. "A guest lecture via video call from the sunny beaches of Morocco. I'll wear sunglasses and a fez for authenticity. Educational and entertaining!"

The dean's mouth twitched, betraying a smile fighting for freedom. "Only you, Hemant, would consider a beachside lecture 'work.'"

"Think of it as... immersive learning," I said, my eyes twinkling with mischief.

Dean Monjolika leaned back, a chuckle escaping her disciplined exterior. "Fine. Go. Teach bartering and beachside economics. But expect an extra faculty meeting on your return."

I stood up, triumphant. "A small price for academic advancement and my family's sanity."

As I left, I heard Dean Monjolika muttering, "Only a finance professor would negotiate a vacation like a corporate merger."

The Term Crisis: More than Just Test Scores

In my class were students, each more bewildered by the day's financial concepts than the last: One student believed 'liquid assets' was a new brand of water; another thought 'bull market' referred to a shopping center for bovines; and a few students were just there because the classroom was the only place with perfect Wi-Fi.

It was the week before the infamous midterm, and the students of Finance 101 were in a frenzy. Among them were an aspiring entrepreneur who believed that "finance" was just fancy talk for "saving money on coffee" and a day trader who thought that reading market trends was as easy as reading a children's book – upside down.

As midterms approached, I announced, "The exam will test more than just your understanding of finance. It will test your very souls!" The class, already accustomed to my hyperbole, barely looked up from their phones. Few in the class exchanged nervous glances. Emma whispered to

Leena, "Is it too late to become an art major?"

The day of the midterm, students found their test papers sealed with wax, bearing my family crest: a calculator entwined with rupee signs. The first question read, "If you had a chicken, two ponds, and a tractor, calculate the net present value of the eggs you could barter for a new tractor." Pari wrote a short story about a chicken who became a tractor salesman. Sagar drew a detailed diagram of a chicken driving a tractor. Bhanu, on the other hand, googled 'egg futures market'.

Halfway through, Arjun started writing poems about fiscal responsibility. Sagar decided to craft a paper airplane. Bhanu, inspired, started calculating the aerodynamics of his pencil case. Leena discovered an online course titled 'Understanding Your Professor: A Guide to Surviving Eccentric Academics'.

As time was called, I collected the papers. "You have all shown me something today," I declared. "And that is... creativity knows no bounds, not even in finance!"

When grades were released, each student found personalized feedback: Pari's story was praised for its narrative flair; Sagar's diagram was called a "masterpiece of accidental art"; Bhanu received a commendation for resourcefulness. The actual finance content? Well, that was a lesson for another day.

Ultimately, 'The Midterm Crisis' became a legend at Pathsala University, a tale of how one unconventional finance exam tested the limits of creativity, patience, and the enduring mystery of my wardrobe choices.

I sat sipping my coffee in a faculty lounge that had seen better days and far too many budget cuts. The lounge, an eclectic mix of mismatched chairs and coffee-stained tables, had become the unofficial arena for the most intriguing academic discussions – and the most amusing.

It was a day like any other, except it was Friday, and everyone knew that the cafeteria served its infamous mystery casserole on Fridays. I, avoiding the culinary gamble, sat with my packed lunch and a pile of midterm papers that looked more depressing than the last stock market crash.

"Hemant, those papers look like they've been graded by a bear market," quipped Dr. Adam, with a knack for timely humor.

"Oh, these?" I sighed, waving a paper adorned with more red marks than a failed startup's balance sheet. "Let's just say my students understand finance about as well as a toddler understands calculus."

Dr. Gupta, the maths professor, perked up. "Calculus? Fascinating subject. Did you know—"

"We're not doing this again, Gupta," I interrupted, saving the lounge from a lecture that would undoubtedly bend time itself.

As I lamented over my students' misunderstanding of basic concepts like 'asset' and 'liability,' Dr. Mamta, the Psychology professor, joined the table, her eyes sparkling with the latest gossip.

"Did you hear about the accounting department?" she began her voice a mix of intrigue and melodrama. "Their new software system converted all their financial statements into haikus."

I chuckled. "Well, that's one way to make balance sheets more poetic."

"Speaking of poetic," Mamta continued, "I'm running a creative writing workshop. You should bring your midterm papers. They could use a little... creativity."

Just then, Dean Monjolika entered, her presence commanding silence. "Jayant, I need to speak with you about your midterms. The students are in an uproar."

I groaned. "I guess it's time to face the music – or should I say the balance sheet blues."

In the Dean's office, I was presented with a unique proposition. "What if," the Dean mused, "we turn this crisis into an educational moment? Let's organize a workshop where you teach financial basics through... let's say, storytelling?"

Back in the lounge, I announced my new plan. "Folks, it seems my finance midterms will now be a storytelling workshop. Imagine 'Scam 1992' telling the story of Harshad Mehta being enacted by my class.

The faculty burst into laughter. Dr. Nirma, the marketing professor, nodded approvingly. "Now that's a copywriting I'd like to witness."

Next Wednesday, a curious gathering unfolded in the faculty lounge of Pathsala University, where the aroma of strong coffee mingled with the scent of old books. Along with me were present Dr Nirma, a marketing guru known for her colorful presentations; Professor Adam, the economics theorist with a penchant for esoteric analogies; and Dr. Mamta, the psychology expert who enjoyed analyzing her colleagues more than her students.

One brisk autumn day, the conversation turned to the dreaded end-term season. "You know," I began, stirring my coffee slowly, "I've decided to make my end-term exam entirely about hypothetical money. It seems fitting for a finance class."

Dr. Nirma, sipping her chai latte, raised an eyebrow. "Hypothetical money? So, if they fail, they only hypothetically flunk out of university?"

"Precisely," I replied with a smirk.

Professor Adams, whose love for market dynamics was rivaled only by his love for dry toast, chimed in. "That's nothing. I'm considering an exam where the grades are determined by supply and demand. The more students who fail, the higher the value of an 'A.'"

Dr. Mamta, perched on the arm of a sofa, laughed. "I'd love to see the anxiety levels in that class. You'd be single-handedly keeping the campus counseling center in business."

The conversation continued, with each professor playfully one-upping the other with increasingly absurd exam formats. I proposed a finance exam where students invest 'Hemant Dollars' in mock stocks. Nirma suggested a marketing exam where students create a campaign to sell their own test answers. Adams considered an economics exam based solely on theoretical currencies from sci-fi movies.

Finally, Dr. Gupta, ever the observer, said, "You know, we could combine all our ideas. A multidisciplinary exam: invest in your grades, market your answers, and manage your stress. We'll call it 'The End term Crisis: More than Just Test Scores'."

The laughter that followed was interrupted by the dean's sudden entrance. "I hope none of you are serious about these exam ideas," she said, though a smile hinted she was somewhat amused.

"Oh, absolutely serious," I deadpanned as the others nodded in faux agreement.

As the dean left, shaking her head, we returned to our coffee and banter, the stress of end-term season momentarily forgotten in the shared camaraderie of absurd academic humor.

In the hallowed halls of our university, the faculty lounge was a battleground where academic disciplines clashed with the ferocity of a Black Friday sale. One crisp autumn day, as end terms loomed like a tax audit, I sat with my colleagues: Professor Nirma from marketing, Dr. Adams of economics, and Dr. Mamta, the resident psychology expert. We were discussing, as usual, which department had the most stressed students.

"Finance students are so stressed; their calculators are seeking therapy!" I declared, sipping my third Filter Coffee of the morning.

"Please," Nirma scoffed, flipping her perfectly styled hair. "Marketing students are brainstorming so hard, I had to install a lightning rod in the classroom."

Adams adjusted his glasses. "Economics students are recalculating their life choices."

Mamta, ever the observer, noted, "You know, this might be an interesting study on occupational stress..."

The conversation took a hilarious turn when I proposed an unconventional solution to the end-term crisis. "What if we switched teaching roles for a day? I'll take psychology, Mamta can crunch numbers in finance, Nirma can draw supply and demand curves, and Adam... well, he can try to sell ice to Eskimos in marketing."

The idea was met with laughter, but we decided to try it, sparking a series of humorous and enlightening mishaps.

I, in psychology, started my lecture with, "Think of the brain as a bank account where memories are investments." Confused students began calculating the interest rates on their childhood memories.

Mamta, in finance, opened her class by saying, "Money, like emotions, can be irrational. Let's psychoanalyze the stock market." Her students looked like they'd just been asked to solve a Rubik's cube blindfolded.

In economics, Nirma attempted to explain the concept of 'demand' by saying, "It's like consumer desire but with more graphs and less charisma." Her students' blank stares could have been featured in an advertisement for confusion.

Adam, in marketing, enthusiastically said, "Selling a product is like explaining a complex economic theory, but with more smiles and fewer yawns." His students started drafting a marketing campaign for his economics textbook.

The day ended with us reconvening in the faculty lounge, each with a newfound respect for the other's discipline and a shared sense of relief that we were returning to our classrooms.

"Maybe our students aren't stressed about the subjects," I mused. "Maybe they're just stressed about us."

We all laughed, the sound echoing through the halls of academia, a reminder that sometimes, the best solution to a problem is a new perspective – and a good laugh.

I was known for my incredibly challenging exams and my legendary inability to remember names, including those of my colleagues. As fate would have it, my forgetfulness would lead to a series of humorous encounters with Dean Monjolika, a woman who prized recognition above all else.

On a crisp Monday morning, Dean Monjolika ambled into my office unannounced. "Hemant, we need to talk about your end-term exams. The students are terrified!" she exclaimed, adjusting her glasses with a flourish.

I, buried under a mountain of finance books, looked up bewildered. "Monika, is it? Do we have a meeting scheduled?"

"It's Monjolika. Dean Monjolika" corrected the Dean, slightly miffed. "And no, but this is urgent. Your exams are causing a campus-wide panic!"

Unperturbed, I chuckled. "Ah, but you see, Mona, panic is the best motivator for learning the intricacies of financial derivatives."

"It's Monjolika," the Dean repeated, her face reddening. "And this is serious, Hemant. The students are petitioning to have you removed!"

This caught my attention. "Removed? But who will teach them about the beauty of compound interest and risk management?"

"Just... make the exam reasonable, Hemant. Please," the Dean pleaded before storming out.

I slightly adjusted my teaching methods in the following weeks, incorporating more real-world examples and less theoretical jargon. However, my idea of a 'reasonable' exam still involved calculating the financial risk of an alien invasion.

On the exam day, students shuffled into the hall with looks of sheer terror. Dean Monjolika, keen on observing the proceedings, found herself seated next to me; I greeted her cheerily, "Ah, Manju, good to see you."

"It's Monjolika," the Dean sighed but decided to let it slide.

As the students sweated over alien invasion economics, a peculiar thing happened. They began to laugh. The absurdity of the scenario, combined with my witty footnotes in the exam paper, turned fear into amusement.

After the exam, the students gathered around me, discussing the exam with an unexpected enthusiasm. Even Dean Monjolika couldn't help but chuckle when a student said, "I'll never look at an alien movie the same way again!"

In the end, the End-term Crisis was averted not by a change in the difficulty of the exams but by a shift in perspective. Dean Monjolika conceded, "Perhaps there's a method to your madness, Prof Gupta."

And I, with a mischievous twinkle in my eye, replied, "Absolutely, I would love to change my name to Gupta, Dean Monjolika."

The next weekend, I found myself in the throes of a classic academic ritual: grading end-term exams. My study, a room normally reserved for the high arts of number-crunching and nap-taking, had been transformed into a paper-strewn battleground.

My wife, Rani, a woman with the patience of a saint and the culinary skills to match, watched this annual event with a mix of amusement and sympathy. "Remember, dear, it's just a test. Not a quest to find the Holy Grail," she teased as she served me my third cup of coffee for the evening.

"Ah, but Rani, these aren't just tests. They are the mirrors reflecting our students' understanding of the complex world of finance," I declared, my eyes never leaving the sea of papers.

My daughters found my predicament hilarious. "Daddy, are you grading or getting graded by the papers?" Jui asked, her eyes twinkling with mischief.

"Yeah, do they give you a grade too, Daddy?" Jia chimed in, her grin was as wide as her sister's.

I looked up, feigning shock. "Why, I never! I'll have you know that these papers tremble at the sight of my red pen."

The girls giggled and scampered away, leaving me to my monumental task. However, not long after, they returned, armed with colorful markers and stickers. "We're here to help!" they announced, their faces beaming earnestly.

"Oh, no, no, no," I started, but Rani cut in, "Let them help, Hemant. They might learn something about finance."

And so, the grading session turned into a family affair. Jui and Jia decorated the papers with stars and smiley faces, occasionally asking, "Dad, why did this person draw a dollar sign with so many zeroes?"

"That, my dears, is called inflation," I explained, trying to stifle a laugh.

Meanwhile, Rani supplied steady snacks, ensuring the mood remained light. As the night wore on, the pile of graded papers grew, as did the family's enjoyment of their impromptu bonding session.

In the end, when the last paper was graded, I looked around at the smiling faces of my family, the room adorned with more stickers and doodles than a kindergarten art show. I realized that while I might have taught my students a thing or two about finance, my family had taught me that sometimes, the best lessons weren't about numbers at all.

"You know," I said, a contented smile on my face, "I think this was the best end-term crisis ever."

Rani, wrapping an arm around me, replied, "Only until next semester, dear."

CHAPTER TEN

GROUP PROJECTS: THE ULTIMATE TEST OF PATIENCE

My greatest challenge yet was supervising group projects in my 'Principles of Investment' class. These projects were not just a test of my students' knowledge, but an epic saga of patience and endurance for me.

It started off as any other semester, with me enthusiastically outlining the project: each group had to create a mock investment portfolio. I divided my class into groups, mixing the eager beavers with the slackers and the dreamers with the cynics. Little did I know, I was setting the stage for a comedy of errors.

Group One: The Overachievers

This group was every professor's dream, at least at first glance. They bombarded me with questions about ethical investing and hedge funds before I could even finish my sentence. However, their overzealous nature led to daily emails seeking approval for their ever-changing investment strategy, turning my inbox into a warzone of notifications.

<u>What's Good</u>: This group displayed a commendable thirst for knowledge and attention to detail.

<u>Suggestions:</u> A little guidance on focusing their energies could help them streamline their efforts and avoid information overload.

Group Two: The Procrastinators

In stark contrast, this group had mastered the art of doing absolutely nothing. Their idea of progress was deciding on a group name, 'The Cash Cows,' a task that took three weeks and two full class periods. My gentle reminders about deadlines were met with nods and empty promises.

<u>What's Good:</u> Their ability to remain calm under pressure is a rare skill.

<u>Suggestions:</u> Introducing structured milestones and regular check-ins could provide the necessary nudge toward productivity.

Group Three: The Mixed Bag

This group was a jumble of conflicting personalities and ideas. One student believed cryptocurrency was the future, another insisted on investing in only eco-friendly companies, and a third just wanted to invest in pizza stocks because "everyone loves pizza." Meetings often ended in debates, with me playing the reluctant referee.

<u>What's Good:</u> The diversity of perspectives is a valuable asset in exploring creative investment strategies.

<u>Suggestions:</u> A lesson in compromise and the art of blending ideas could turn their debates into productive discussions.

The Grand Finale

The final presentations were a spectacle. The Overachievers presented a sophisticated portfolio, albeit with a 300-page report. The Procrastinators somehow pulled together a decent portfolio, though their presentation had the panicked energy of a last-minute all-nighter. The Mixed Bag delivered a surprisingly well-balanced portfolio after finally agreeing to invest in 'eco-friendly pizza.'

<u>What's Good:</u> Each group, in its unique way, demonstrated learning and growth.

<u>Suggestions:</u> Encouraging early and consistent effort, fostering teamwork, and guiding balanced decision-making can enhance future group endeavours.

In the end, I congratulated the students on surviving the ultimate test of patience. "You've learned a valuable lesson," I said, beaming. "Finance is not just about numbers, but also about managing... personalities."

The students didn't know whether to laugh or cry. They had survived my experiment, emerging with not just finance knowledge but life skills in patience and diplomacy. And I? I was already planning next semester's group project – something about international trade and interpretive dance.

As the students filed out, they knew one thing for sure: group projects were indeed the ultimate test of patience. And I, the puppet master of patience, had orchestrated it all with a masterful, if slightly mischievous, hand.

The Moral of the Story

I, sitting in my office post-presentations, reflected on the chaotic journey. I chuckled to myself, realizing that beyond the numbers and analysis, I had imparted a more valuable lesson: the art of working together, a skill more complex than any financial strategy. I reached for my grade book, a small smile on my face, knowing next semester would bring a new set of challenges – and laughs.

My other ultimate test of patience: supervising a capstone group project.

The project was simple: analyze a company's financial health. However, the group was a mix of students from finance, marketing, psychology, and economics, a recipe for creative chaos.

I watched in horror as the marketing students suggested evaluating the company based on the color scheme of their logo. "It's all about brand perception," they insisted.

Then came the psychologists, advocating for a deep analysis of the CEO's childhood to understand the company's financial decisions. "It's all about the subconscious mind," they explained with a Freudian air.

The economists, with graphs in hand, argued for a purely theoretical approach. "Let's assume the company operates in a vacuum," they proposed to the sound of collective groans.

As debates raged and PowerPoint presentations multiplied, my patience wore thin. I longed for the sweet solace of my spreadsheets and number-crunching.

In a desperate bid for peace, I sought advice from my colleagues.

The marketing professor suggested a brand makeover for the group project itself. "Give it a catchy name and a logo," she said. Professor Nirma, with a smile as shiny as a new ad campaign, had a suggestion. "Hemant, darling, make it about branding! Have them create a marketing campaign for the company. Numbers are dull, but everyone loves a catchy jingle!"

I chuckled, imagining my serious finance students crafting jingles about fiscal policies.

The psychology professor advised on group dynamics. "Perhaps an exercise in trust falls would enhance cohesion," she recommended, probably half-joking. Dr Mamta, known for her insightful understanding of the human psyche, had her own idea. "Hemant, it's all about group dynamics! Make them analyze the company's culture and leadership style. Finance students need to understand people, not just numbers."

I mused over the idea of my students psychoanalyzing fictional CEOs instead of crunching numbers.

And the economics professor simply stated, "Let them reach an equilibrium. It's the invisible hand of group work. Hemant, it's simple. Incorporate macroeconomic trends. Have them predict the company's growth in different economic climates. That'll keep them busy."

My head spun with these colorful suggestions. The Capstone Project was becoming less about finance and more about jingles, Freudian analysis, and climatic economics.

Armed with this eclectic advice, I returned to my students. I combined the suggestions into a master plan, creating a project that was part brand analysis, part psychoanalysis, and part economic theory - with a dash of finance.

The project commenced, and chaos ensued. One group created a jingle so catchy it went viral in the university, but their financial analysis was as shallow as a kiddie pool. Another group psychoanalyzed their fictional CEO so thoroughly they diagnosed him with an Oedipus complex yet couldn't balance a budget. The third group got so caught up in economic forecasts they started a heated debate about Keynesian economics, forgetting the project entirely. The presentations were so uniquely bizarre that it left the entire faculty members speechless. Charts analyzed the CEO's choice of pets alongside market trends. The logo's color palette was correlated with fiscal stability.

In the end, I learned an invaluable lesson: group projects were not just a test of patience, but also a wild journey through the interdisciplinary landscape. I also made a mental note to never seek advice from my colleagues again - at least not all at once.

As for the students, they learned that finance wasn't just about numbers but about the colorful, sometimes absurd world of interdisciplinary collaboration. And me? I have a story to chuckle over for years to come, usually over a well-deserved cup of coffee, far away from any group projects.

One day, Dean Monjolika approached me with a grand idea. "Hemant," she said, twirling her hair that was as meticulously groomed as my portfolio, "I've been thinking. Let's spice up your MBA class with group projects! You need to lighten up with these group projects and make it Fun. It's the ultimate test of patience!"

I, who believed fun in finance was a perfectly balanced spreadsheet, was skeptical. "Fun, Dean? The only 'fun' in finance is the 'F' you get for not balancing your sheets." But I reluctantly agreed.

The day arrived. I announced the group project with a smile as forced as a bullish market on a bad news day. The students formed groups like clusters of stocks in a volatile market - some blue-chip pairs, a few speculative ventures, and one group that was the equivalent of junk bonds.

As the groups delved into their projects, I observed the chaos with a mix of horror and amusement. One group, "The Diversified Portfolios," couldn't agree on anything, resembling a board meeting more than a study group. Another, "The Bull Runners," had ambitious ideas without grounding in reality, like investing in tulips during the 1630s. The Group, nicknamed "The Procrastinators," believed deadlines were merely suggestions. Their leader once tried to turn in a paper during graduation. The Group, "The Overachievers," led by Arjun, had enough enthusiasm to power a small city. They wanted to start their project three weeks before it was assigned. The Group, "The National Coalition," struggled not with finance but with deciding whether their meetings would be in English, Hindi, or interpretive dance.

My patience was tested daily. I caught "The Procrastinators' printing their project during the marketing class's midterm exam. Arjun sent me seventeen emails in one hour, each with a slightly different version of their spreadsheet. 'The National Coalition,' meanwhile, decided their project would be best presented as a finance-themed musical.

Dr. Monjolika, upon seeing the chaos, offered her suggestions:

"Team Building Exercise!" - She suggested an ice-breaking session where each member shared their favorite stock. The result was an hour-long debate about the merits of investing in tech vs. traditional industries.

"Regular Progress Reports!" - This led to groups creating PowerPoint presentations that were so elaborate they would make annual shareholder meetings look like a casual chat.

"A Motivational Speech!" - I gave a speech about teamwork and synergy, using as many financial puns as possible. It was met with eye-rolls and confused looks, but at least one student chuckled.

Surprisingly, the groups pulled together on the day of the presentations. The Diversified Portfolios managed a balanced analysis, and even The Bull Runners grounded their ideas in realistic financial strategies. The musical was a bizarre yet insightful spectacle about the rise and fall of various economies. The team mascots, ranging from a plush Rupee bill to a small cactus named 'Spike the Budget Balancer,' became beloved class icons.

Much like the stock market, I learned that group projects are unpredictable but can yield surprising results. I also decided to stick to lecturing and leave the motivational speeches to those with less affinity for spreadsheet humor.

And Dr. Monjolika? She realized that sometimes, the best investment you can make is in a good laugh and letting things take their course. "After all, isn't that what the Efficient Market Hypothesis is all about?" she remarked. I was horrified at this explanation of the Efficient Market Hypothesis but did not correct my boss.

I sat at the dinner table with Rani and our two daughters. The topic of group projects had come up, and I, in my usual professorial tone, began to discuss it as if I were lecturing in a hall full of eager students.

"Now, you see," I began, swirling my spaghetti thoughtfully, "group projects in finance are not just about crunching numbers. They're an intricate dance of personalities, a true test of patience and human endurance."

Rani glanced at her daughters and winked. "Is that why you always look like you've just survived a battle after grading them?"

Jui, my older daughter, chimed in, "Yeah, Dad. Last week, you said you'd rather explain Algorithm Trading to a cat than read another poorly done project."

Jia, my younger one with a mischievous glint in her eyes, added, "And let's not forget the group names. 'The Fiscal Four,' 'Dynamic Depreciators,' 'The Audit Avengers'..."

I sighed, "Ah, yes, the names. It's like a parade of puns and financial wordplay. But beyond the comical exterior lies the real challenge – collaboration. In the real world, finance is all teamwork, and these projects are a miniature reflection of that world."

Rani nodded sagely, "A reflection that apparently includes someone always disappearing, someone doing all the work, and someone who just adds their name at the end?"

"That's eerily accurate," I admitted. "And each plays a vital role: the ghost group member who tests your ability to handle uncertainty, the overachiever who challenges your delegation skills, and the name-signer, the ultimate test of your patience and forgiveness."

Jui, pondering my words, said, "So, it's not just about finance. It's about managing people?"

"Exactly!" I exclaimed, delighted. "Finance, my dear, is but a backdrop to the grand theater of human dynamics."

Jia, grinning, asked, "So, Dad, which one was you in college? The ghost, the overachiever, or the name-signer?"

My eyes twinkled as I replied, "Ah, well, that's a story for another day. But let's just say I learned much about patience myself."

As the family laughed and dinner continued, the topic shifted, but the lesson remained: group projects, in finance or otherwise, were indeed a test of patience, a lesson in human nature, and occasionally, a source of family entertainment.

CHAPTER ELEVEN

Final Lectures and Farewells: Leaving a Legacy

I stood at the head of my dinner table to practice my farewell speech. Rani and our daughters, Jui and Jia, sat in the front, armed with popcorn and expectant smiles.

"Ladies and gentlemen," I began, adjusting my glasses, "today, I won't bore you with numbers. Instead, I'll share three life lessons that are absolutely free – no tuition necessary!"

Rani rolled her eyes playfully; she had heard my dad's jokes for decades.

"Lesson one," I continued, "always invest in relationships. They give the best returns. Case in point: my marriage. I proposed to Rani with a ring I bought at a discount. I calculated the cost-benefit ratio, and well, the benefits have far exceeded the costs!"

The girls laughed. Rani blushed, mouthing, "At least he admits it."

"Lesson two," I went on, "diversify your portfolio. Like I did with my daughters. I wanted one to follow in my footsteps, but they both became artists. Now, I invest in both stocks and art supplies!"

Jui and Jia exchanged amused glances. Their art projects had always been an alien concept to their finance-savvy father.

"Finally, lesson three," I said, "Know when to retire. It's like understanding market trends. You don't want to sell too early or too late. For me, it's the perfect time. I'm selling high – I still remember my login password and haven't called a student by my dog's name this week!"

The girls erupted in laughter. Rani wiped a tear, half from laughter and half from pride.

Rani and my daughters engulfed me in a group hug.

"Dad, that was hilarious!" Jui exclaimed. "Who knew finance jokes could be funny?"

"And to think you were worried about being too dry," Jia added, grinning.

Rani smiled, looking up at me. "You always were the best investment I ever made," she said.

My eyes twinkled behind my glasses. "And you, my dear, are the dividend that keeps on giving. I will now start preparing for the final lectures. My audience might not be able to relate to this advice"

My family knew that though my lectures might be getting over, their adventures were just beginning – with laughter as their constant companion.

For my students, I wasn't the ordinary finance guru; many called me a legend. It is not just for my uncanny ability to explain the complexities of hedge funds while juggling tennis balls but also for my notorious end-of-term lectures, which were as unpredictable as the stock market on a caffeine high.

As the semester drew to a close, whispers filled the corridors. This wasn't just any final lecture. This was the Grand Finale, the Big Adieu, the Last Hurrah—I was retiring.

On the day of the semester's final lecture, the amphitheater was packed. Economics majors, business enthusiasts, and even a few lost art students who had heard the rumors and didn't want to miss the show. At precisely 10:00 AM, the lights dimmed, and a spotlight hit the stage. There stood I, dressed in a suit that seemed woven from Rupee bills, a twinkling bowtie, and shoes that looked suspiciously like repurposed gold bars.

"Welcome to the ultimate lesson in Finance 101," I began, my voice echoing dramatically. "Today, we learn about... leaving a legacy!"

I clicked a remote, and the screen came to life with a graph labeled 'Banerjee' Impact on Student Sleep Patterns.' There was a notable spike around exam times.

"The first rule of leaving a legacy," I continued, "is to ensure you're unforgettable." I unveiled my first surprise—a life-size cardboard cutout of myself, complete with a voice box that spat out classic Banerjee quotes like, "Inflation is the only thing that keeps me up at night, besides my dog, Dollar."

The lecture continued with a series of increasingly bizarre stunts. There was the 'Budget Balancing Act,' where I balanced the department's budget on the nose of a trained dog named Fiscal. And who could forget the 'Derivative Dance-Off,' where I challenged the Economics Department Chair to a break-dance battle to explain market fluctuations?

But the pièce de résistance came at the end. "To truly leave a legacy," I said, pulling a cover off a mysterious object, "one must invest in the future." Underneath was a shiny new coffee machine labeled 'The Banerjee Expresso.' "For all those late-night study sessions. May your investments be as strong as your coffee."

As the students applauded, I took a bow. "Remember," I said, my voice tinged with a rare seriousness, "finance isn't just about numbers. It's about life, laughter, and learning. Go out there and make your mark!"

And with that, I, who taught everyone that finance could be fun (and occasionally absurd), left the stage. My legacy? A generation of students who understood that the value of knowledge, like the best investments, only grows over time.

As the day of my retirement approached, whispers and wagers proliferated across the Faculty of Economics, Marketing, and Psychology, each department curious about my final series of lectures for the university.

The Finance department expected a solemn summary of fiscal theories, but I had other plans. My lecture was a comical yet insightful journey through economic history, depicted through a series of hilarious skits involving notorious figures like John Maynard Keynes and Milton Friedman in imaginary sitcom scenarios. Students and faculty rated this swan song a solid 10/10 for both education and entertainment.

The Marketing department, always keen on branding and image, prepared a glossy, over-the-top retirement brochure, complete with exaggerated claims of my 'market impact.' To their surprise, I launched my own guerrilla marketing campaign. I plastered the campus with humorous flyers, praising my 'rival' marketing professors for finally recognizing the superiority of finance. The marketers couldn't help but chuckle at the playful jab, giving it an 8/10 for creativity and a 9/10 for execution.

The Economists, with their love for models and theories, expected me to present a detailed analysis of the economic impact of my retirement. Instead, I delivered a mock economic forecast that predicted a sharp decline in 'campus humor indices' and a 'bear market in faculty fun' post-retirement. My colleagues in Economics rated this unexpected twist a 9/10 for humor and a 10/10 for originality.

The Psychology department, interested in the emotional aspects of farewells, anticipated a reflective discourse. I, however, presented a tongue-in-cheek analysis of the 'stages of grief' my colleagues would supposedly undergo after my departure. I even handed out 'Banerjee Coping Kits' filled with humorous self-help pamphlets. The psychologists found this both amusing and endearing, giving it a 10/10 for thoughtfulness and an 8/10 for psychological accuracy.

In conclusion, my final lecture series, Masterclass in Humor and Wit, left a legacy of laughter and learning. My colleagues from the varied disciplines were united in their admiration and amusement, realizing that beneath the playful exterior was a brilliant mind that had profoundly impacted them all.

My final lecture series to the finance students included:

- "The Economics of Goodbye." I entered the hall dressed as a wizard, declaring I was off to join the "Economic Council of Elders." I spent the hour explaining the fiscal impact of retirement plans using a "Gandalf the Grey to Gandalf the White" metaphor. Students were both amused and bewildered.

- "Inflation and the Incredible Shrinking Rupee." I brought a balloon, inflating it until it popped. "Like this balloon," I bellowed, "our economy can only handle so much hot air!" The students, used to my eccentric methods, just nodded, picking bits of balloon out of their hair.

- "Risk Management: The Art of Not Falling Downstairs," was an interactive obstacle course. I turned the lecture hall into a mock 'Financial Danger Zone,' complete with slippery 'stock market' floors and 'budget deficit' hurdles. It was a lesson in physical and fiscal balance.

- But it was the final lecture that left the biggest impression. Titled "The Wealth of Knowledge: Investing in Futures," I took a more solemn tone. I spoke about the value of education, the investment in oneself, and the returns of sharing knowledge. I concluded, " Today, I won't lecture on financial models or investment strategies. Instead, I will share the greatest secret of finance". The room fell silent, everyone eager to hear this revelation. "I see the future financial leaders of the world gathered here. Remember, it's not about how much you earn, but how much you can make others believe you've earned". The room erupted in laughter.

Then, I announced, "For my last act, I've prepared a special assignment." I handed out papers that looked like a complex new type of financial analysis. The students groaned, but their expressions changed to amusement as they started reading. The assignment was a series of humorous yet insightful questions such as, "Calculate the NPV (Net Pizza Value) of a pizza shared among friends," and "If you invest in a winery, does the ROI (Return on Intoxication) justify the expense?"

The participants were in stitches. One student asked, "Is this going to be on the final?" I winked and replied, "Only if you can solve it while balancing a budget on a unicycle."

The lecture ended with a surprise. Each student received a personalized ledger, inside which were notes from me on their strengths and how they could leave their own legacy in the world of finance.

As the lecture ended, students lined up to bid farewell, thanking me for the lessons and the laughs. Some even attempted to answer my quirky assignment questions.

Years later, hopefully, my legacy will live on. Former students, after turning into successful financiers, might often recall my teachings, especially the importance of humor in the face of financial challenges. I will want them to remember me not just as a finance professor, but as a mentor who taught them that even in the serious world of finance, there was always room for a good laugh.

I was also invited to address the students of the other different departments before leaving.

The marketing department, always ready to brand anything that moved, had already begun designing "Banerjee Farewell" merchandise. T-shirts with my face and the slogan "In Finance We Trust" were a hit, especially among students who never quite understood my lectures but respected my fashion sense.

During my last lecture to the marketing students, I decided to incorporate their lingo. "Think of the stock market like your social media strategy," I began, "unpredictable, often based on whims, and when it crashes, it does so spectacularly." The marketing students, for the first time, nodded in complete understanding.

The economics department had always viewed me as a peculiar enigma. "He treats finance like it's a form of art," complained Professor Adam, "and everyone knows money is far too serious for creativity."

In my farewell lecture to the economics students, I decided to prove a point. I began discussing "Fiscal Policy and Impressionism," drawing parallels between economic theories and various art movements. "Like Monet's lilies, a well-balanced portfolio requires a mix of texture and light," I mused. The economics students left the lecture confused yet oddly inspired to paint.

The psychology department had always found me fascinating. They wondered what made a man so passionate about numbers tick. In my final lecture, I decided to delve into the psychology behind financial decisions. "Our relationship with money," I began, "is like any romance – thrilling at first, then complicated, and before you know it, you're considering a prenup."

I went on to explain behavioral finance, a topic I'd never touched before. The psychology students were captivated, scribbling notes furiously. My lectures, usually a tranquilizer, had suddenly become as thrilling as a psychological thriller.

At my farewell party, the faculty from all departments gathered, still baffled but now bemused by my unconventional methods. They presented me with gifts –

a painting from the economics department, a marketing campaign for my upcoming book (tentatively titled "Stocks and Bonds: A Love Story"), and from the psychology department, a detailed analysis of my personality.

As I looked around at my colleagues and students, I realized my ultimate investment had paid off. I had not only taught them about finance, but I had also left a legacy of laughter and a new perspective on an old subject. And as for me, I was off to my next adventure, armed with spreadsheets and a newfound love for puns.

I recalled all the fond memories of my colleagues from different departments in the faculty lounge. The Marketing Professor Nirma, a woman so charismatic she could sell sand at the beach. Professor Adams, from Economics, could calculate the GDP of a country just by looking at its lunch menu. And from Psychology came Professor Mamta, known for analyzing people's dreams better than they could remember them.

"My dear colleagues," I announced, "today, we merge our disciplines in a grand last experiment!" I unveiled my master plan: a mock economy where each department had to use its skills to create the most profitable venture. The catch? They had to use Monopoly money, and the winner would receive the prestigious Golden Ledger Award.

Professor Nirma immediately launched a marketing campaign for 'Mamta's Psychic Services' - a venture that combined Mamta's dream analysis with investment advice. Ever the strategist, Professor Adam began trading resources with such efficiency that even the Monopoly banker was impressed.

Meanwhile, I orchestrated the event with the glee of a child at a candy store. I walked around with a Monopoly top hat, making witty remarks and throwing in financial puns that made even the dullest accountant chuckle.

As the game progressed, alliances were formed and broken, trades were negotiated, and laughter filled the room. My final experiment turned into a roaring success, a blend of education and entertainment.

In the end, it was a close call, but 'Mamta's Psychic Services' won by a dream. Professor Nirma, grinning from ear to ear, accepted the Golden Ledger Award, promising to display it proudly in the Marketing Department's trophy case.

As the event came to a close, I took a moment to reflect on my career. I thanked my colleagues for the memories, reminding them that "in the grand ledger of life, it's not just the assets, but the memories we create, that truly matter."

I decided to bid farewell with a speech tailored to each department.

I began, "Dear marketers, you who can sell sand in the desert and ice to Eskimos. I've always admired your creativity in making people buy things they don't need with money they don't have. Remember, without your strategies, the world would never know they needed a Bluetooth-enabled toothbrush!"

Laughter erupted as the marketing professors, who indeed could sell a ketchup popsicle to a woman in white gloves, appreciated the humor.

Next, I turned to the economists. "Ah, economists, the only people who will see light at the end of a tunnel and still argue if it's an oncoming train or the exit. Your forecasts are admirable, often reminding me of weather predictions - equally unpredictable and equally confident!"

The economists chuckled, acknowledging that predicting the economy was indeed as tricky as nailing jelly to a wall.

Finally, I faced the psychologists. "And to you, the mind-benders. You understand why a man standing on a frozen lake gets cold feet, both literally and metaphorically. Remember, while you analyze the madness of the masses and the sanity of the solitary, keep in mind that every time you find an answer, human behavior changes the question."

The psychologists nodded, amused and fully aware of the complexities of the human psyche they dealt with daily.

As I concluded, I said, "As I leave, remember, the world of academia is a bit like a ledger. Every debit has its credit, and every theory has its critique. But the balance we create – knowledge, understanding, and a few laughs along the way – is what truly counts."

There was a hearty round of applause for me as I stepped down, leaving a legacy of laughter, learning, and a reminder that in the grand scheme of things, we're all slightly absurd entries in life's great financial statement.

The Professors had kind words for me.

Dean Monjolika tapped her glass, signaling the beginning of the tributes. "When I first met Hemant," she began, her voice laced with mischief, "I thought he was the embodiment of the 'Time Value of Money' – he always looked like he'd rather be anywhere but at a faculty meeting. But seriously, Hemant taught us all something invaluable – that finance isn't just about numbers; it's about life. And for that, we reluctantly forgive him for making us recalibrate our entire grading curve!"

Dr. Nirma stepped up next. She cleared her throat and began, "When we first heard that Professor Banerjee was retiring, we in the Marketing department wanted to launch a campaign: 'Keep Banerjee – He Makes Financial Sense!' But alas, here we are."

The audience chuckled as Dr. Nirma continued, "Hemant, you've taught us all so much about finance. Why, just last week, I finally understood that 'liquid assets' aren't just fancy cocktails. Your ability to simplify complex financial jargon has been a gift – like when you explained 'bull and bear markets' using our faculty cafeteria's Chicken Briyani and Dal Khichadi days."

Next came Dr. Adam from the Economics Department. He adjusted his glasses and said, "We economists are known for our, ahem, 'thrilling' personalities. But next to Professor Banerjee, we're a veritable circus. Hemant, you have the unique talent of making supply and demand curves sound more sleep-inducing than a lecture on the history of watching paint dry."

The crowd erupted in laughter as I chuckled, my eyes twinkling behind my spectacles.

Next came a younger professor whose modern theories often clashed with my old-school approach. "Professor Banerjee and I didn't always see eye to eye – especially when I suggested cryptocurrency as a course topic," he started, drawing a hearty laugh. "But there's no denying the impact he's had. His dedication to his students was unparalleled. He didn't just teach them about finance; he prepared them for life. He was the only one who could turn a lecture on compound interest into a life lesson about patience and growth."

Lastly, Dr. Mamta from the Psychology Department walked up. "As a psychologist," She began, "I've always been fascinated by Hemant's mindset. He has an uncanny ability to remain calm in any financial storm. I once asked him how he manages his stress. He said, 'Easy. I just imagine my investment account growing – works better than therapy and is cheaper, too!'"

Dr. Mamta paused for effect, then added, "We've analyzed Hemant's behavior and concluded that his love for numbers is borderline obsessive. In fact, if he were any more obsessed with numbers, we'd have to consider him a prime candidate for our next case study."

As the speeches concluded, I stood up, my eyes gleaming with mirth. "Thank you for your 'invaluable' insights," I said with a grin. "I'm just glad I'm retiring before I became the subject of a psychological experiment or an economics model gone wrong. As for Marketing, let's just say I'll miss the creative interpretations of my finance courses!"

The faculty gave me a standing ovation for the experiment and the years of wisdom and wit I had imparted. My final experiment wasn't just a farewell but a celebration of a career spent enriching minds and tickling funny bones.

And so, I exited Pathsala University, leaving behind a legacy of laughter, learning, and a slightly confused Monopoly banker wondering how the economy had turned into such an entertaining affair.

CHAPTER TWELVE

CAPS, GOWNS, AND SURPRISING SENTIMENTS: GRADUATION DAY

On the auspicious day of graduation at Pathsala University, I stood out in my vibrant purple gown, starkly contrasting to the usual dark suits that cloaked my lean frame during finance lectures. My gown, a little too long, made navigating the sea of graduates an adventurous, albeit perilous, endeavour. *I have been called out of retirement to attend this Graduation Day.*

"Watch the gown, folks! It's a rental!" I bellowed, as I nearly tripped over a jubilant graduate snapping a selfie.

Leena, one of my brightest students, approached with a grin. "Professor Banerjee, I never imagined I'd see you in anything but tweed!"

"Ah, Miss Leena," I retorted with a theatrical sigh, "finance isn't just about predictability and trends. Sometimes, you've got to expect the unexpected!"

Leena chuckled, "Like expecting my student loans to magically disappear?"

"Only in a perfect economic model, my dear," I winked, continuing my precarious journey.

Next, I encountered a student who often dozed off in class. "Awake and in broad daylight! What's the occasion?"

The student rubbed his neck sheepishly. "I wanted to thank you, Professor. Your lectures were so... soothing. I had the best naps."

I feigned shock. "Well, I hope you've invested in a good alarm clock for the real world!"

As laughter echoed, Bhanu, notorious for his risky investment strategies in class simulations, joined the group. "Professor, remember when you said I'd either end up a millionaire or penniless with my stock choices?"

"Indeed, I recall preparing you for the rollercoaster of Dalal Street," I nodded.

Bhanu beamed. "I took your advice, played it safe, and... well, I just bought my second startup!"

"Ah, my lessons veered you towards the conservative path! I'm surprised but delighted!" I exclaimed, momentarily forgetting the perilous length of my gown.

Finally, I encountered Emma, a quiet but insightful student. "Professor Banerjee, I'll miss your classes. You really made finance... less daunting."

My heart swelled. "Thank you, Emma. That means more than you know."

As the ceremony began, I took my seat, my gown sprawling theatrically across the aisle. My hawk-like gaze, usually reserved for spotting errors in balance sheets, now observed the graduation ceremony with a mix of bemusement and bewilderment.

Beside me, Dr. Nirma, the marketing guru with a penchant for colorful metaphors, whispered, "Hemant, you look like you've just calculated the probability of each of these graduates paying off their student loans."

Ignoring her quip, I adjusted my own cap, which sat on my head like a reluctant cat on a vacuum cleaner. I scanned the crowd and remarked, "I just don't understand the need for such pomp and circumstance."

Professor Shamay, the elderly history buff whose stories often lacked an ending, chuckled. "Hemant, it's about celebrating the end of an era. Like the fall of the Roman Empire, but with less drama and more confetti."

As the procession began, the finance department found themselves in a less-than-strategic position behind the ever-enthusiastic physical education faculty, who were performing what could only be described as calisthenics to the tune of 'Pomp and Circumstance.'

"Look at them, will you?" I muttered, "You'd think they were warming up for the Olympics, not a graduation."

Dr Mamta, always quick to find humour, replied, "Well, considering the length of these ceremonies, a bit of a workout might not be the worst idea."

As names were called and diplomas handed out, my stoic expression softened each time a finance major walked across the stage. I whispered calculations of their GPAs and potential career earnings, a proud and somewhat peculiar display of affection.

This graduation day, I was also asked to give the graduation speech. I was more comfortable with spreadsheets than speeches. My sudden assignment to give the graduation speech was, in student circles, considered an act of administrative humor.

The students, dressed in their caps and gowns, whispered and wagered how many would remain awake during my speech. Even the faculty had a betting pool going, though they'd never admit it. Everyone braced for an oration drowned in fiscal theories and compound interest anecdotes.

But today, I surprised them all. I stepped up to the podium with a mischievous twinkle in my eye, a sight as rare as a balanced budget in a startup company.

"Good afternoon," I began, in my trademark tone. The audience settled in for a long nap. But then, something unexpected happened. I donned a pair of outrageously glittery glasses. "Let's talk about the ROI of your education—but not in the way you're thinking."

I proceeded to deliver a speech filled with the most uncharacteristic wit and humor. I compared the stock market to dating—"volatile and unpredictable, but with patience, you might just hit the jackpot." I likened tax codes to mystery novels, "dense, often boring, but full of unexpected twists."

The students were in stitches. Who knew I had such a comedic side? I even made a joke about debits and credits that had everyone roaring with laughter, a sentence no one thought would ever be spoken.

As I concluded, I took off my glittery glasses and returned to my usual serious self. "But remember," I said, adjusting my cap, "life is more than numbers. It's about the risks you're willing to take and the memories you make. So go out there and diversify your portfolios of experience!"

The crowd erupted into applause, a standing ovation for the most unexpected comedy act of the year. Caps flew into the air, and I, a small smile on my lips, quietly left the stage, my job done.

As I stood amidst a sea of black caps and gowns, I was approached by a group of students. My spectacles were perched precariously on my nose as I clutched my notes looking as out of place as a penguin in a desert.

"Professor Banerjee!" called Arjun, one of my brightest students, who approached with a grin. "I finally figured out the real-world application of the Black-Scholes model!"

"Excellent!" I exclaimed, only half-listening as I tried to calculate how many seconds until the ceremony was over. "Does it involve calculating how fast one can leave a graduation ceremony?"

Before Arjun could respond, Sagar, known more for his partying than his portfolio management, swaggered up. "Professor, I'll never forget your advice. Buy low, sell high. Changed my life."

I raised an eyebrow. "Sagar, that's the equivalent of remembering to breathe."

As more students gathered, sharing memories and gratitude, I found myself oddly touched. Maybe, just maybe, there was more to my job than balance sheets and bear markets.

I cleared my throat and prepared to impart a final nugget of financial wisdom. But looking out at the hopeful faces, I said, "Remember, the best investment you can make is in each other."

The students erupted in applause, surprised by the sentiment from the man they thought only knew the language of ledgers. I smiled, my heart swelling a bit—though I'd never admit it.

As the ceremony concluded and the graduates tossed their caps into the air, I found myself clapping the loudest. I turned to my ex-colleagues; my usual gruffness softened by a rare, genuine smile. "Maybe there's more to these ceremonies than I thought. Like a well-diversified portfolio, it's a mix of tradition, celebration, and... well, just a bit of silliness."

Dr Mamta laughed, "And just like that, the Sultan of Spreadsheets becomes the Philosopher of Finance."

We walked back to the department office, caps slightly askew, gowns billowing, and hearts unexpectedly light. For once, the numbers weren't the most important thing on my mind.

I said a final goodbye to my ex-collegues and sat in my car. As I drove my ancient, trusty sedan – fondly named 'The Bull' – I reminisced about my career. My mind was a ledger of memories, balancing humor and wisdom with impeccable precision.

Just as I was musing over a particularly funny incident involving a calculator and a helium balloon, my car sputtered and coughed. 'The Bull', it seemed, was not as eager for retirement as its owner. Stranded on the side of the road, I did what any self-respecting finance guru would do – I called for a tow truck and calculated the cost-benefit analysis of this delay.

While waiting, a peculiar sight caught my eye. A small, roadside stand, proclaiming 'The World's Most Accurate Fortune Teller'. Intrigued and having time to spare, I decided to partake in this financial anomaly.

The fortune teller, a sprightly old woman with eyes as sharp as bear market claws, greeted me. "Ah, a man of numbers and logic. Let's see what your future holds," she said, her fingers dancing over her crystal ball like stock tickers on a trading floor.

She peered into the ball and declared, "I see... I see... a great investment opportunity!" I raised an eyebrow, skeptical yet amused. "Indeed? In what, pray tell?"

"In rest and relaxation!" she exclaimed. "Your greatest gains will now come from investing in hobbies, laughter, and maybe even a bit of gardening."

Chuckling, I thanked the fortune teller and tipped her with a rare, out-of-circulation 1000 Rupee note, a collector's delight.

Finally, the tow truck arrived, driven by a young man who looked as if he had just embarked on his own financial journey. As we drove to the nearest garage, I imparted unsolicited yet invaluable advice on compound interest and diversified portfolios.

The delay, however, had a silver lining. I found myself at a quaint café I'd never noticed before. Over a cup of steaming coffee and a spoonful of Bhel, I struck up a conversation with a fellow retiree, an ex-art teacher with a penchant for colorful scarves and abstract painting.

As the sun set, painting the sky in hues of gold and orange, I realized that retirement was not the end of my ledger but an exciting new chapter. I might have closed my textbooks, but the world was still ripe with opportunities to learn, laugh, and, perhaps, dabble in a bit of gardening – just as the fortune teller had advised.

With a smile, I drove 'The Bull' home, ready for the adventures that lay ahead in the unpredictable market of retired life. And, as I always told my students, in the great stock exchange of life, diversification is key.

I reached my quaint home. I parked the car, patting it affectionately. "Well, we've diversified our assets today, haven't we?"

Inside, I kicked off my shoes, tossed my academic cap onto the sofa, and looked around. Retirement awaited, filled with unknowns, but like a good investor, I was ready to embrace risk for the potential of high returns. I have Rani and the girls waiting for me.

Rani poured me a glass of fine aged wine and toasted "To new beginnings, unpredictable markets, and life's uncharted ventures!"

As night fell, I sat by my window, a book in hand, smiling at the stars. Retirement, I realized, wasn't the end of my story. It was just an exciting new chapter, a fresh page in the ledger of my life, waiting to be joyously balanced.......

www.ingramcontent.com/pod-product-compliance
Lightning Source LLC
Chambersburg PA
CBHW031136130726
47988CB00006B/2395